JAKE SLATER: REVENGE OR RETRIBUTION?

JOHNNY GUNN

WOLFPACK PUBLISHING
— EST 2013 —

WOLFPACK
PUBLISHING
— EST 2013 —

Published in the United States by Wolfpack Publishing, Las Vegas

Wolfpack Publishing
6032 Wheat Penny Avenue
Las Vegas, NV 89122

wolfpackpublishing.com

Paperback ISBN 978-1-64734-969-1
eBook ISBN 978-1-64734-968-4

JAKE SLATER: REVENGE OR RETRIBUTION?

1

The freshness of the spring air at sunrise had Wes Trimble wide awake and ready for another day of branding and doctoring a growing herd of cattle. He and his wife stood on the top step of his kitchen porch looking out across the broad spread of his ranch, stretched out in a valley west of the Ruby Mountains. "Look at that, Dorothy, it's all ours and spread over several hundred acres of grass, brush, gullies, and stunted cedar. A man would have a hard time wanting more than this," he said.

The morning mist carried the rainbow as it rose to greet the dawn. Buckaroo dust was sprinkled with brilliant diamonds. Spring in the high mountain desert of Nevada sings and paints, but ever so quietly.

"It's been a long fight, old girl, but we're winning. Boys are 'bout growed up, don't got much coin, but we got this. Went hungry a time or two, but that's behind us." His shoulders, broad as a barn's big doors, never slumped, his eyes never cried, and it's only been in the last few years that he was able to smile, for real, not just to make Dorothy feel good.

She rested her head on his shoulder and tried her best to get her arm all the way around his waist. "It's been a hard life, Wesley, but one filled with love and warmth. You're a wonderful man."

Trimble was a large man in every respect. Tall, heavy, and strong enough that men rarely challenged him, even when he wasn't carrying that big Remington or razor sharp Bowie. The knife was made for him by his teenage daughter, Jennifer, and it hadn't been properly tested. Yet.

Dorothy on the other hand was described as petite, standing barely five feet tall and weighing an amazing ninety pounds. Despite her diminutive size, Dorothy had delivered three children, two boys and a girl, and in that order. Jennifer was almost fifteen years old, and almost as petite as her mother.

"Boys lit out earlier with Sam. Throw together something for me to eat while I'm in the saddle, Dorothy. I'll go join them, moving some of them high priced critters into the high ground today. Others as the week works on."

"I wish you men took more time in the morning to eat, like you used to. It was better, Wes."

"I think you're right, but you and Jennifer, even working together, can't do it. Maybe if we have a good year, we can hire someone to run the kitchen. Been kind of lean the last few."

Dorothy chuckled as she put a sack of food together to stuff in saddlebags. It was ready by the time Wes Trimble had his horse saddled and bridled. She smiled as she watched him ride off and he waved back at her as he rode north to find his foreman and sons. He didn't have to go far. He saw the dust of three riders coming on hard and pulled up to wait for them.

"Tore out a whole line of fence, Dad," Frank Trimble said. "Looks like they ran off with about a hundred head. Heading north best I could tell."

"No!" Trimble's whole body trembled at the words, as anger, fear, and frustration raced through him. "How many?"

"Think maybe four riders, Boss," Sam Overton, ranch foreman said. "Must of been late at night. Me and the boys were out there plenty early. Got a good start on us."

"All right, let's ride 'em down. We get anywhere near another ranch or Skelton, one of us will ride for help. Can't afford to lose a hundred head. My God, no." Trimble growled his anger and motioned for them to move out. It was just him, Sam, and the boys running his herd and he depended on those fences. He couldn't afford to hire buckaroos to ride with the cattle. When he sent them into the hills for the summer, Sam and the boys went with them. But it wasn't time yet. They were still in winter pasture, safe, behind good fences.

Sometimes I could just cuss this life of ours. We could see daylight, almost, and now this. A hundred head? My God, why not just burn us out, too. The harder they rode the more the anger built, the more the potential loss set in. "We put those fences in tight, boys. Sunk those posts deep."

"They pulled them cedar posts right out of the ground, Pa." George Trimble was sixteen, almost as big as Wes, and carried the unfortunate nick name of Wuzzie, mostly because of his hair which seemed to have a million tight curls that had never been controlled. "Dragged the wire clear and trailed them steers right on out."

The trail they left was more than obvious and the four riders followed at a steady fast trot for several hours. It led them into the Ruby Mountain foothills, northerly and into rocky country. The Ruby Mountains stretched north and south from the Western Pacific Rail lines, to Eureka, with peaks topping twelve thousand feet. They were riding along the western face, which gets the most water every year.

"Skelton's just a few miles west of us, Pa. Think we should get some help?"

"No, we got to be close now, Frank. Let's keep going. We've got a good pace going, horses are fine, and lots of daylight left." Wes Trimble was not going to lose his herd. He'd been fighting nature, Indians, and now had to face rustlers. "I'm not letting them go. I give and give and give, and I ain't giving no more."

"They're pushing that herd hard," Sam Overton said. "I first figured they stole them steers after midnight but I'm thinking now, it must have been just about sunset. I don't think we're catching up." Overton was a Texan by birth, had made several drives north before coming west and joining up with Wes Trimble. In his mind, this would be the last brand he'd be working for.

"Look," Wuzzie yelled. He was pointing at thin threads of dust maybe two miles in front of them. "Gotta be our beef."

The four were at a full gallop through stands of aspen and pine, around and over the rocks of the foothills, in and out of gullies, and rode hard on three men driving the stolen herd of beef. The rustlers saw them coming and spread well out, pistols drawn. A fourth rider was with the cattle leaders and picked up his pace, knowing gunfire would erupt soon, and he would have running cattle.

The three rustlers dove behind a stand of rocks to make their play. The one with a rifle watched the four riders coming hard. "I'm gettin' one of 'em, for sure," he said.

Wes Trimble and his son Wuzzie were leading the charge and Wuzzie took a rifle slug high in his chest, which threw him down into the hard rocks. Wes pulled up instantly, as did his son Frank. Sam Overton continued the chase until the three outlaws put all their fire his way. He turned back before they found the range.

"Wuzzie, no, no." Wes howled his grief, jumping from his horse and racing to his son's side. "Frank, ride hard for Skelton. We need help. Ride, boy." He knelt at Wuzzie's side, heard a moan, breathed a deep sigh, knowing the boy was alive. "Get a fire started, Sam, and some water on. He's alive. Those men will pay dearly for this."

No, no, no. My son? My herd? My life? No. The sobs were as silent as he could make them as visions of everything he and Dorothy had built slowly ebbed away. *I won't lose my son, and I won't let those men take my herd. So help me, I won't.* His gnarled hands were clenched so tight he could have bent steel and his mind was just as determined.

"It's all right, boy. We gotcha, and we ain't losin' you. Hang on, boy, hang on."

2

Richard Burdick was the Elko County resident deputy in Skelton and was about to enjoy a cold beer, late on a beautiful spring day. He was with Valley Paddock, the village's postmaster and business man at the Alabama House Saloon. Horseface Hawkins was behind the long plank, telling another long and involved war story from the great war between the states. He had fought on the losing side but you'd never know it from his generous stories.

"Well, well," Paddock said. "Ricky Burdick come to visit, are you?"

"They call it spring, Valley, but it feels more like July out there today. I'll take a large mug of the coldest you have, Mr. Hawkins, and be ready to fill it again. You be heading out to Slater's place for the doins? Gonna miss it this year. Sheriff wants us all in Elko for a talk about the rustling that's been goin' on."

"I'm heading out mid-day tomorrow. Got some good beer and bourbon to bring. Ain't like you to miss a big feed like this, Ricky Burdick." Hawkins cackled loud and long.

"Save me a chunk of Slater's beef, Horseface, but gotta stop this rustling."

"There's something fishy smellin' about this rustling, too," Valley Paddock said. "Keep hearing that they ain't no rustling, just fence busting. That sheriff of yours smart enough to get it stopped."

"Well," Burdick said, and let the question drop. "About the fences, though, that would mean they be a bunch of cattle out there on the range just roaming around. No, Valley Paddock, they be rustling cattle. They be bustin' fences in order to rustle cattle. They ain't just turning good beef loose, no sir."

Valley Paddock couldn't understand how these men were able to steal herds of cattle and be able to get rid of them. "Who's buying all this stolen cattle, Rick? Why all at once is there a market for stolen cattle? None of this makes any sense to me. I'm a business man, I think a pretty good one, and I don't see the profit in this. Steal it and get away with it, fine, but why did you steal it? To sell more than likely. So, who's buying all this stolen cattle?"

"Too many questions for me to answer," Burdick said. "Maybe finding that answer is what I should be doing, though."

"I don't think your sheriff's up to it," Paddock said.

The heavy door of the Alabama House was flung open and Frank Trimble, eighteen, rushed in. "Burdick, come quick. Wuzzie's been shot, rustlers got our herd. Come quick." He shouted, panting from the hard ride into town.

"My God," Burdick said. "Where is Wuzzie? Where's your father."

"We was chasing the rustlers north from the ranch. They're just a few miles east, Burdick. Wuzzie's hurt bad and them foul outlaws is gettin' away."

Rick Burdick ran out to his horse, followed by Frank Trimble and Valley Paddock. "Get a group together and follow us," Burdick yelled to Paddock. "Let's go, Frank." It was a hard three miles up into the rocky foothills of the Ruby Mountains and both horses and men were breathing hard when they found Wes, his wounded son, Wuzzie, and the foreman, Sam.

"He's alive, Burdick, but my herd's gone, now. Take Frank and Sam, and chase those men down. Save my herd, Burdick, please. I can get Wuzzie back to town. Go, man."

Rick Burdick nodded, motioned for Frank and Sam to follow, and rode out at a hard trot. "How far in front, Sam?"

"Got another good hour on us, Rick. Don't know if we have enough day left to catch 'em.

There's four of 'em, and they all have rifles."

"We'll catch 'em," Frank said. "We'll catch 'em good and put some hurt on 'em, too."

Burdick kept the hard pace for another couple of hours before they saw heavy dust in the air more than two miles in front of them. "We can be there before dusk, boys," he hollered. "They must not think they're being followed, going as slow as they have been. Got one chance, boys, that's all, before these horses collapse on us." He changed the pace to a faster lope and the three rode hard for the beckoning dust.

Lather flew from the racing horses and the three men only saw dust in front of them as they made their way through the jumble of the Ruby Mountain foothills. One misstep, one turned rock, and horses would tumble, breaking legs - kill riders and each man knew it. But the thought of letting these cowardly outlaws run off with Trimble's herd made them ride hard.

The springtime sun was doing its best to stay above the horizon, but the men could feel evening coming on hard. They'd lose them sure once it got dark and the rustlers must know that. They could keep moving the cattle in the dark because they wouldn't give a darn if some got hurt. "We're close," Burdick said. "Watch for riders, not cattle." Burdick was riding with buckaroos and knew their first thoughts would be to their herd, not to the men who would kill them on sight.

The drag rider saw the posse coming hard and yelled for the others. They scattered into nearby outcrops of Ruby Mountain granite and tall trees, their rifles at the ready. "Kill 'em all, this time," one yelled, diving into the dirt. "Gotta get this beef taken care of tonight."

Burdick motioned Sam Overton to his left and Frank Trimble to his right and jumped from his horse, running as hard as he could for a stand of pine trees. He heard one bullet sing its nasty song whipping its way past his ear and dove for cover. The outlaws were uphill from him and had a better view than he did. He squirmed around in the dirt and brush and got a nice view of one outlaw trying to get a bead on Frank.

"Uh, uh," Burdick murmured. He eased the rifle hard into his shoulder and put just a touch of pressure to the trigger of that monster Henry he carried. When the whitish smoke cleared there was a dead cattle rustler sprawled in the rocks. Sam Overton took that moment to run ten yards to another chunk of rock and dove behind it just as two bullets ricocheted off it.

"Too old to try that again," he growled. He eased around the rock and spotted the two men who shot at him. A quick shot from the Winchester knocked one of them down and the other returned fire immediately, hitting Overton in the arm. Sam reeled back behind the rock and ripped his bandanna off to stem the blood. "You ain't killin' me, mister."

"How bad?" Ricky Burdick yelled over.

"Gonna live," Overton hollered. "And that fool ain't."

Two quick shots rang out from Burdick's right, and were followed by a howl of pain. "Got one, Burdick," Frank yelled.

"Nice and easy now, boys let's take 'em out. Start shootin' and move forward slow and steady." He eased out to the side of the pine he was behind and heard a horse racing off. He stood up, looked around quickly, and ran hard for the rocks the outlaws were hiding behind. There was no gun-shots. Sam and Frank joined the charge.

Two of the outlaws were dead, but one was alive, though bleeding hard. "We'll try to save your rotten hide, mister. But the other half of the deal is, you tell us who's behind all this."

"Ain't gonna tell you nothin," the man said. He coughed up blood, his eyes were dull, and he was too weak to sit up by himself.

"Well, we'll still try," Burdick said. "Find their horses, Sam, and we'll get the dead loaded and do what we can for this fool. Frank, can you get that herd of yours put together by yourself before it gets too dark to find 'em?"

"On my way," he said.

Valley Paddock led three men on the trail north after meeting Wes Trimble bringing his wounded son into Skelton. "I alerted Doc Whitney that you'd be coming, Wes. You know where he lives? How's that boy?"

"He's hurtin', Valley, but I got the bleeding stopped, I think. I know Whitney's, and thanks," he said.

"Let's go men," Paddock said. He, blacksmith Jesse Winthrop, and The Lady Nevada Saloon owner Jose Torres rode off to find Burdick and the rustlers. "We've got daylight on our side, boys." He chuckled, looking at the sun, sinking fast. He set a strong pace riding along the tracks left by the cattle and Burdick's men. "Can't be that far in front of us."

It was at least two hours when Torres tried to call a halt. "Shots," Valley yelled. Paddock was well in front of the small posse. "Lots of shootin' not too far in front of us." They rode out fast and reached Burdick in minutes.

"Glad you're here, men. I just sent Frank out to gather the herd and I know he'd welcome some help."

"I'm fair at that," Winthrop said and rode off right away.

"Where's Sam?"

"Gathering the rustlers' horses. One got away. Sam took a round, but I think he'll be fine. Don't know if there are any others or not, but we got this one, still alive. The two dead ones are over there. See if you know them? This wounded one is a stranger to me, and ain't talking about his partners."

"Don't know him, either," Paddock said. He walked over to the two bodies and gave them a long look. "The one in the red shirt's been in the store a couple of times. Don't recall a name though."

"Ever mention who he worked for?" Burdick hollered.

"Somebody south, I'd say. He rode in from the south each time, I think. That could be any of five or six outfits." Paddock knelt down and went through both men's pockets, coming up with some double eagles, but not much else. "This one carries a fine knife, but no identification. No paper of any kind. I've got a note from someone, though, from the other feller."

He handed the note to Rick Burdick, who read it out loud. "It says, 'Meet us in Elko after.' That's it. Nothing else."

"After?" Paddock said. "What? After they stash the herd somewhere? Something to go on, anyway."

"Don't want to ride back in the dark, so let's set up camp and ride in in the morning. Sam, how's that arm? You good for the night?" Sam grunted, nodded that he was fine, and to prove it grabbed some firewood.

"Hope Frank and Jesse can keep the critters controlled. Cows should be plenty tired after todays run." Burdick knew he was tired. "I'm gonna have a few things to tell the sheriff at our meeting tomorrow. It would be nice if I could tell him something more about these men."

"What would be nicer, Rick, would be if you could tell him why they stole the beef," Valley Paddock said. "They got to sell it to somebody. They were moving it north, into more ranching country, mostly fenced. This ain't west Texas, Rick. Why are they taking beef?"

Burdick couldn't answer, Sam's arm hurt so he didn't even try, and Valley finally quit pacing around and helped get a good fire going. "Somebody better figure it out."

3

Frank Trimble and Jesse Winthrop brought the Trimble herd right through the middle Skelton late the next morning, and were met in front of Valley Paddock's Emporium by Wes. "The most wonderful sight in the world, Frank. Wonderful." The weight of not knowing if his son would live, if his herd was gone, all lifted with the dust and clamor of a herd moving through town.

"How's that ugly brother of mine?" Frank yelled out.

"Gonna be fine, son. Gonna be fine."

Burdick and Paddock rode up to the front of Paddock's store, leading three horses, two of which were adorned with bodies. The wounded man was also laid out across the saddle and tied down. "Better get this one up to the Doc's, Valley" Burdick said. "I don't know why he's still alive. I gotta send some wires off to the sheriff. He's gonna want to know about this right away."

"You still planning to head for Elko for that meeting?" Paddock had the lead rope and was ready to make the short ride to Doc Whitney's.

"Even more so, now," Burdick said. "Tell the doc to watch out in case this fool tries something stupid. Never trust an outlaw, no matter how much he hurts."

"You need help driving that herd back to its home pasture?" Jesse Winthrop hadn't spent this much time in a saddle in years and his rump and knees were telling him so. "Give me a hot fire, hard anvil, and a big hammer over a saddle any day of the year."

Wes Trimble was laughing, watching the big man climb down from his horse. "I think we can manage, Jesse, but I do want to say thank you for helping. Come by for a steak dinner any time you're in the area."

Sam Overton had ridden to Doc Whitney's as they rode in to get his arm looked at, so wouldn't be riding south with the herd. "I'll take drag," Wes said and his oldest son, and the only other drover around, Frank Trimble got the leaders moving, knowing the rest would follow right along. "Wuzzie's gonna be fine and so is Sam, Frank. It's just us, son. Let's go home."

"Let's see what we can do about these bodies, Jesse." Valley Paddock said. "Gonna be a warm one today and don't need that problem."

"By the time we get 'em buried it'll be time to head out to Jack Slater's feast. Looking forward to that. He'll be glad to know these rustlers are dead and wounded."

"You sound like you believe these that we caught are the whole gang? I don't believe that for a minute, Jesse. Like I said earlier, who is buying all this beef that's being taken? There has to be a market or why bother?"

"I guess you're right, Valley. I ain't got no answer."

Day five of branding week at the Slater Ranch, some five miles outside Skelton, Nevada, and the dust was hanging heavy in the air. The aroma of cattle, horses, fresh grass, hot steel, and burnt hair flowed through the spring time air along with the voices of buckaroos cussing, whooping, and crying out. Sweat poured in gallons and mixed freely with the dust.

Most buckaroos had to argue with themselves over which was more beautiful, birthing season or branding week. Absolutely the hardest work they would have over the year and the most fulfilling. Nicks from the knives, scabs from the burns, gloves worn out from singing ropes, and a grand party to call it a week.

Robbie Slater was working as one of the ground men while his father Jack was heeling and dragging calves to the fires. Cactus Jack Faraday was helping to drive the branded calves back to the holding corrals so they could find their mamas, while half a dozen buckaroos kept things moving along. There's no more busy time on a ranch than branding time.

There was an abundance of activity with three fires going, buckaroos cutting young ones, others working on the ground, and the fences filled with friends and family. Maybell, nearing seven years now, was with her brother, Henry Seth, almost four, cheering every time their father made a good heel shot.

Everyone called the boy Seth, the name in honor of Seth Bullock, he of Deadwood in the Dakota Territory, who had helped Jack so many years ago. "Good, Papa." He yelled and laughed, hanging onto the bottom rail of the corral fence. He had tried to wiggle through more than once and Maybell was getting frustrated trying to keep him in line.

"You stay outside the fence, now, or I'll take you back to the kitchen," she scolded. Seth couldn't control his eagerness to be a part of the activity and broke free to scamper into the mass of whirling horses, running calves, and slightly agitated mama cows. He made a bee-line for Jack's horse after Jack had heeled a feisty calf, which was almost free of the lariat.

"No!" Robbie Slater saw his young brother make the dash, dropped his knife, and dove headlong for the boy. He wrapped him in his arms and tried to roll away from the calf, now several hundred pounds of escaping energy. Jack Slater let off on the rope's tension and the calf stepped free of the loop to race away, stepping onto and across Robbie.

"You boys okay?" Jack sprang from his horse, gathering his rope. "What's Seth doing in the corral anyway? Maybell, where are you?" Slater was looking to thump someone. How many times had he told the kids to stay out of the working corrals. "Maybell," he howled.

Maybell was having a hard time getting through the corral rails, crying. All work in the branding yard came to a halt. Jack got Robbie and Seth untangled and on their feet, picked Seth up to make sure he wasn't hurt, put him down and marched him to the fence. "You, young lady were supposed to be watching him. Now, Seth, you go with your sister, back to the house. And you, Maybell, keep him there."

Jack Slater wasn't yelling, in fact, his voice was soft, simply telling the children what they were to do. The buckaroos, standing around watching all this, had a different take on the matter. Cactus Jack fully understood that the softer Jack spoke, the more angry or worried he was. Several of the men simply looked at each other, or away, grinning, wondering if Seth would get away with this encroachment without a spanking.

"Now, Maybell," Jack said. "Take Seth by the hand and go back to the house and stay there." He stepped back in the saddle, shook out a loop, and looked for a calf. The men held in their chuckles and got back to work in a hurry because all that worry could turn to fury in a flash. "Back to it, boys, the day's gonna pass us by."

There were no other more exciting times on most ranches than branding and Jack Slater's ranch always brought in people to help. There were surrounding ranchers jumping in to help, day help people came in from near-by towns and villages, and everyone waited for the end of the day when tons of good food were eaten.

Great tubs, half filled with ice were strategically placed for the mountain oysters which would be sliced, rolled in flour and deep fried, some roasted, others pickled, and eaten with the exuberance of the day. The women folk and older children seemed to be just as busy as the men in the corrals.

The spring crop of calves had been good and from the word being spread around the various valleys in Elko County, many of the ranchers were looking at a bounty year. Robbie Slater, the adopted son of Jack and Mims and now, newly married, was more than pleased since being named cowboss the year before.

Robbie was exceptionally bright, had been schooled by Mims and Jack, and was taking courses in animal husbandry, by mail, from a university in Chicago. He was specializing in breeding, knowing the background of the bulls used, and how heifers had performed. He used everything he'd learned in his breeding studies for the Slater herds. "We've got a nice looking crop, Papa. When we're through with the branding and tagging, we'll get them out to pasture."

"Looks like we made the right moves buying that bottom land out there," Jack said. Their ranch was on the western flanks of the Ruby Mountains. The town of Skelton sat at the base of the mountains and the Slater place sloped out about five miles west. The home place sat on a quarter section that Jack bought when he first arrived in Elko County several years ago. Since, he has picked up two sections and turned them into pasture. He planted and cuts winter feed, too.

Many of the surrounding ranchers took their herds into the Rubies for summer forage, which was loaded with good grass, but not every year. Jack rotated his herds through their own lands and had dug several irrigation ditches that distributed water across the fields. The area was blessed by generous winters, most years, with heavy and deep snow piling up in the high peaks of the Ruby Mountains.

"There are several ranchers more than upset with the way some of us are running our herds, Dad. We bought that land and they think it should be open range. Amos Warren is making a lot of noise about fences and irrigation. Talking about tearing out fences."

"I've heard some of the talk, too, Rob. Warren's foreman, Sonny Belafleur is trying to get things all worked up. We'll be having a cattlemen's meeting in Elko later this next week to air some of these problems. Why don't you and Cactus Jack ride in with me. After this week we can use a day rambling around."

"Mama's gonna want to come along, you know," Robbie laughed. He caught himself up quickly, frowned, and said. "My wife, Liz, too, I expect."

"Be good for all of us." Jack was laughing, watching his son learn the ways of being a married man. "You'll never get used to it." *Lord knows I never have. Mims surprises me more often than I want to think about. Has from that first day on the Jablonski Farm.* He often thought about that morning when he saw Mims, ten-years-old, as he was, come out onto the porch and almost take command. *I'll never stop loving that woman.*

4

"I'm either getting old or we have too many cows." Jack Slater wiped dirt and sweat from his face, took a long drink of cold water, and leaned against the corral fence. "What's the tally, Cactus?"

"Well over four hundred steers, some nice looking keeper heifers, and just a few early market animals." Cactus Jack Faraday had a smile on his grimy face, giving Jack the totals from several days of branding. The long, tall Texan leaned back in the saddle, stretching his legs out to the side. "We ain't old, Jack, but we got parts and pieces showing some wear."

"I think we earned our keep this week," Slater laughed. "Better get the big fire started cuz I think that dust cloud out there is Horseface Hawkins coming our way with a barrel or two of beer."

It had become a tradition at the Slater ranch to cap off branding week with a fire roasted steer and barrels of beer. Beans, fresh baked bread, and as many pies as the women could bake, topped things off. Often there would be music and some of the buckaroos would have girlfriends from town join them. "Got a nice fat steer already on the spit Jack and a tub of ice from the ice house for the beer."

"One step ahead of me, eh?" Jack Slater gave his foreman a good look right in the eye. "Been together a long time, Cactus. Remember how upset old Ted Wilson was when I stole you away from his ranch?"

"Worse than that, Jack, I remember getting the daylights beat out of me and this place burned to the ground that first year." Cactus Jack almost died from the attack and still carried scars.

"Nobody will ever burn me out again, Cactus. It was at that moment you changed from being my foreman to being a member of the family. I know I'm a crazy man when it comes to family, but it's the only thing that means anything in my life. To this minute I still miss my parents."

Jack Slater had lost his parents in a buggy wreck in New York when he was ten and as an orphan, came west on the orphan trains. They brought children to needy families in the farming west. He landed on the Jablonski farm in Dakota Territory and grew to the man he is today, needing a safe, warm, and loving family.

"You got one now, Jack." Cactus Jack couldn't hold back the chuckles. "You came to Nevada alone, looking to build a ranch. Now, you got four kids, a wife, a daughter-in-law, and me. You, sir, are a family man."

Cactus Jack had been ranch foreman from the first week that Jack Slater owned the ranch, and was known as the finest cow man available in all of Nevada. "With what Robbie has learned and put into practice, about breeding, we've got one fine beef herd, Jack. We'll get top prices again this year." He looked around at the crew, making sure everything was where it was supposed to be.

"We need to have a talk about some of the things that big-mouth Sonny Belafleur has been saying about people putting fences across open range. The man's a serious trouble maker."

"Let's enjoy this party tonight," Jack said. "You and Robbie be with me in the morning. We'll go over all the figures and make plans for the season. There's a cattleman's meeting next week in Elko. I've already told Rob about it and I want you with me, too. Amos Warren and his crew have been getting a little too pushy for my blood."

Robbie rode up alongside the two. "Must be Horseface coming in, Dad. That's more dust than just his team and wagon. I'm taking the cattle back out. Be back soon."

"No, it's just Horseface," Jack laughed. "He drives like the devil's chasing him and is about to snare him up. Stand back now, cuz he don't like to stop them chargers."

Horseface Hawkins brought his team, along with a cloud of dust, to a sliding stop at the corral fence. His gimpy leg didn't slow him down a whit, and he baled from the wagon seat with a grin from ear-to-ear. "The big barrel's full of golden beer, Jack Slater, but I've got a smaller keg tucked away down here. What's in this has been there long enough to start school, come June. Right out of my own still," he cackled.

"I've got some good and bad news, too," he said. "Four yahoos rustled Wes Trimble's herd and almost got away with it. Three of 'em are dead, one should be, and the herd's on its way home."

"That is good news, Horseface. Did anyone recognize the outlaws? Hope this means an end to that problem. Lost too much good beef," Slater said.

"Nobody knows 'em," Hawkins said. "Valley Paddock said one of 'em's come into his store a time or two, though. Ain't none come into the Alabama House."

Horseface owned the Alabama House Saloon, made the finest Bourbon west of the Rockies, and would talk your ear off if given half a chance. He fought for the south in the big war, still suffered from many war inflicted wounds, and was one of the first residents in the town of Skelton, Elko County, Nevada.

"Valley Paddock will be along shortly, Jack. Where's that pretty bride of yours. I want to make sure I'm on Mims's dance card." Hawkins was laughing loud as he handed down a keg of bourbon.

"She and the kids are in the house, Horseface. Go on in, we'll take good care of these fine kegs of yours. Got ice for the beer keg and tin cups for the smaller one."

Three buckaroos lifted the big barrel out of the wagon and rolled it into the barn and got it settled in a water tank filled with chopped ice. They spread a heavy layer of straw over the ice and laid a canvas sheet over the straw. "That'll keep cold long enough for us to get it drank," Two-dog Sorenson laughed.

Cactus Jack hefted the Bourbon keg and carried it to tables set up near the cooking fires. "Might as well test it, eh, Jack?"

"Must, Cactus. We must," Jack said. "Robbie should be along shortly. He, Andy Pettigrew, and Tiny Howard rode out to move the last of the cattle out to pasture."

They watched Wanda Camacho slowly turning half a beef on the spit, Robbie's new bride, Elizabeth, was stirring a huge cast iron kettle of beans, and

Maybell, was trying to get a log, half her size, onto the fire. Wanda started to help and Maybell let her know she could take care of it. "I've got it, Wanda."

Valley Paddock, the postmaster and owner of a large general merchandise store in Skelton, rode up with a couple of others from town, in for the party. It didn't take long for most of the beef and beans to be eaten, all of the beer drank, and most of the bourbon gone. Empty pie plates were being gathered.

The stars were sprinkled as a bright warm blanket across the sky when the party finally broke up. Many who came slept under their buggies and wagons, some slept in the barn, and a few romantic couples were seen to edge into the woods, near the stream.

"Glad that's over for the year." Mims chuckled, putting her arms around her big husband's shoulders. They were in the upstairs bedroom listening to the quiet. "We'll just nest up here for the rest of the spring." She could already hear Jack's gentle snore and kissed his shoulder good night. "To think I fell in love with this monster when I was ten-years-old."

Breakfast was an ordeal as Mims, Wanda, and Elizabeth simply made platter after platter of bacon and hot cakes, bowls of fried potatoes, onions, and peppers. There were gallons of coffee for all who spent the night. It was ten in the morning before the tide of visitors ebbed and quiet reigned in the Slater kitchen. "They all gone, Mama?" Maybelle asked.

"Lordy, I do hope so," Mims said. "We do this every year and every year I say we'll never do it again. Maybe if I don't say it, we won't." She had a mug of coffee and found a chair at the long table. "Sit with me, Elizabeth. You must be worn out, too."

"I am, down to the bone, Mama Mims, down to the bone. What's up with the men? They have been in with Jack all morning. Robbie has come out twice for pots of coffee."

"Jack wanted to get all the figures in the books while they were fresh, he said. They'll be out soon. We'll let them get that mess outside cleaned up. I bet there isn't a pound of beef left on those bones. Hogs will be in heaven for the rest of the day."

"One of the best years we've had," Jack said. "That deep grass of ours and a little finishing come fall, and we'll do all right."

"Will if we can fend off the fence busters," Cactus Jack said. "I've also heard a rumor that there's more to this than just wanting to run cattle on the open range. The thing with Amos Warren and his group is, they don't think they have any responsibility to the open range. Just put the cattle out there."

"That idea went down the spout years ago, Cactus," Robbie said. "Most of the ranchers are coming around to understanding the concept of sustainability, but not Warren and his group."

"That's part of the rumor I heard last night. Seems that most of the fence busting is done at night and often, instead of someone running their cattle in on the good pasture, they're running the well fed cattle out and making them disappear." Cactus Jack had an angry look on his thin, almost drawn face. "Using the fence busting to rustle, is what I've heard."

"Think old Amos Warren's behind that?" Jack Slater took a quick look out the window. "That fat old man doesn't have that kind of thinking, Cactus. Besides, those four rustlers who hit the Trimble place are dead or wounded. Don't know if that means the rustling will end, but Warren isn't smart enough to do what's being talked about."

Jack took a long drink of coffee and stood up for a stretch. "I think we need to take a ride down to the Trimble place and have a talk with Wes and his boys. That man's had some struggles but he's winning. Might need some good words from us. We might just learn something."

"You're right, Jack. Amos Warren isn't smart enough to run a rustling gang, but that foreman of his is. That's something that Sonny Belafleur would surely think of." Cactus Jack looked out the window. "Valley Paddock said they tried to run off with more than a hundred of Trimble's cattle."

"Gotta have a market for something like that," Robbie said. "Sure can't run branded cattle through the feed lot sales. Where would you sell those cattle?"

"South," Jack Slater said. "Rail heads being put in near Caliente, south of Pioche. Could move cattle to southern California, or east for that matter. Let's keep all this to ourselves at the meeting and just listen. It would be a long drive south, plenty of time to alter brands, and a waiting market."

"Glad I won't be making that drive," Cactus Jack laughed. "You want to bring anyone with us when we visit Trimble?

"Yeah, let's bring Two Dog Sorenson. And," Slater said with a crooked smile across his weathered face, "let's ride close by Amos Warren's place. Not on it, don't want to be rude, but close, eh boys?"

5

The spring morning carried a hint of the coming summer heat as the four men rode out from the Slater ranch. "There's open range this side of the Warren ranch that we can cut through to get us close to Amos's place and still be headed to Trimble's," Jack Slater said. "Might want to look around some for traces of a large herd moving through."

Gentle laughter filtered through the dust as they turned south and rode through Skelton. "Ten or fifteen years ago, rustling around here was to build you a new herd," Jack reminisced. "Trimble's cattle were not stolen to build a new herd. They were stolen to be sold and I agree with what you said earlier, Rob. Who's the buyer?"

Warren's property was about four miles south and west while the Trimble place was about four or five miles past that. They moved off the main road and walked their horses through open range, covered in new greenery from grass, sage, and other brush. There were scattered stands of cottonwood near water sources, with piñon and cedar spread around some.

The rolling and undulating range sloped gently from the more rugged Ruby Mountain foothills into a long and broad valley. "Warren never tried to buy an acre of this beautiful country," Jack Slater said. "But he demands to be able to run his cattle on it anytime he wants. Something we might want to talk about at the meetings next week, Rob. Making sure there's enough open range, making sure we don't ruin what we've got. They talk about that in your books?"

"You bet, Dad." He was looking off into the distance, not really paying attention to his father. "Got some riders coming up. Two for sure, about two miles out." Rob Slater pointed off to the south at some distant plumes of dust. "Looks like they're at a solid lope to me."

"We're not on private property, but let's not start something, either," Jack said. "If Sonny Belafleur is with them, you keep yourself under control, Cactus."

"I will until he don't, Jack." Cactus Jack Faraday had more than one run-in with Belafleur, in town, on the range, and at meetings. The bad blood started when Belafleur suggested that Cactus Jack had cheated in some way at a buckaroo gathering at the Skelton fair grounds. There are those that still talk about the fight that took place, with Cactus Jack the winner and Belafleur bleeding badly.

"Man called me a cheat, Jack, and got whipped for it. Not man enough to let it go at that, and I'm telling you right now, I won't start anything, but I won't be prodded, either."

"Fair enough," Slater said. They rode in silence, watching the two riders close on them. "Looks like Belafleur and Toby Forbes. Let's spread out a bit, boys, just in case. Forbes is a nasty little man. Wasn't he prodding you, Two-Dog, at the fall sales?"

"That's him, Jack. Like Cactus, I'll be easy like." Two-Dog Sorenson was the oldest of Slater's hands, but also one of the handiest with pistol and rifle. He was a crack shot with both. Generally considered the easiest to get along with, many also remember a few times when he wasn't.

The two riders rode right up to the Slater group before pulling their mounts to a stop. "This is Warren range, Slater. You got no business here." Sonny Belafleur had his rifle across the saddle and his hand near his sidearm.

"This is open range, Sonny and you know it. I'll ride through open range any time I want and you're in no position to tell me otherwise. You got something else to say, say it. Otherwise, move aside, Belafleur." He nudged his horse into a walk, straight at the Warren ranch foreman.

Belafleur had two choices, pull on four men and die or move aside and let Slater and his men through. "I better not find you moving Warren cattle, Slater," Belafleur snarled.

"Wouldn't want a Warren beef mixed in with mine, Sonny. We breed up, not down. Don't suppose you know anything about that rustling over at Trimble's?"

"Haw," Belafleur shouted, spurring his horse and riding off at a full gallop with the other Warren hand.

"Oh, Jack," Cactus laughed. "You hurt his feelings."

"Morning, Wes." Slater hollered out as the four rode into the barn area. "Thought we might talk about that mess you got into."

"Jack Slater. This is a pleasure. Yes, sir, it was a mess indeed. Step down and let's find some coffee. Robbie, you've grown another foot since I saw you last. How's married life, son?" Trimble took their lead ropes and helped hold the horses as everyone dismounted.

"Never been better, Mr. Trimble. Wuzzy getting healed up?"

"Can't keep that boy down. You going to the meetings next week, Jack? I got a few things to say. Don't know yet what those yahoos were planning for my beef when they run 'em off. Where you gonna sell branded beed?"

"We've been asking the same questions, Wes. You ever have a run-in with Amos Warren or that outlaw foreman of his?" Slater asked. "Belafleur just tried to tell me I wasn't allowed to ride across open range."

"Hope you laughed right in his face, Jack. I looked closely into the faces of those men that stole my beef and I've never seen any of them before. Now, Jack, think about that for a minute. Four men never seen in this country cut my fences and run off with a hundred head of branded cattle. That don't make no kind of sense."

The conversation lasted through two full pots of coffee before Jack Slater said they better head on back home. "We'll talk some more in Elko, Wes. Outlaws have never been known for their incredible intelligence, but stealing cows and not being able to turn the deed into money is serious stupidity. If we find their market we can find them is the track I'll be taking." They mounted up and waved back at Trimble and Dorothy.

"Let's ride boys, and on the way home maybe we'll ride a little closer to the Warren home ranch. Belafleur's got me prodded now, Cactus."

"You're the boss and you know we'll cover your backside, Jack. Did you notice how Two-dog Sorenson was smiling and talking sweet to that Trimble girl? She's kind of young for you, ain't she, Two-dog?" Cactus Jack was laughing and pointing at the man.

Jennifer Trimble turned fourteen over the winter and was tall and very pretty. "She's a sweet young girl, Cactus, and we have a lot in common. You were so busy eating all those sweet rolls you didn't even see the knife she showed me. Sides, I'm only thirty."

"Only! I won't be thirty for years to come," Cactus said.

"You might not make thirty if you keep prodding that feller," Slater laughed. "What about that knife?"

"She made it, Jack. On her father's forge, using her father's tongs and hammers. Made that beautiful knife. Better than the ones I make and you know how good mine are." Two-dog's knives were well known on the Slater ranch. Almost everyone carried one and proudly so.

"Well, then, Two-dog, I stand corrected," Cactus said. "Maybe you and Jennifer should go into into the knife making business."

"Comin' up on a Warren fence," Rob pointed out. We gonna ride right along the fence line?"

"Yup," is all Slater said. "Wes said his cattle were driven north east from his fenced pasture, so it would have been well away from Warren's. Looks like we got company coming our ways, boys. Nice and easy does it, now."

Amos Warren and Sonny Belafleur rode up on the Warren side of the fence line. "Looking to cut fences, Slater?"

"Wouldn't think of it, Amos. And, good morning to you, too." The snide remark washed right over Warren and Jack continued. "Talking with Trimble about the meetings next week and the rustling going on. If you were to steal a hundred head of beef, where would you sell them?"

"You come one step on my property and you're a dead man, Slater." Warren jerked his horse around and the two rode off at a gallop.

"That was the best prod yet, Jack. You're getting good at it," Cactus Jack laughed.

Amos Warren was rotund, sloppy fat in some minds, and had a dreadful hatred of men who were fit, successful, and had families. His father, equally obese, died of a heart attack when Amos was ten, and his mother always blamed the successful businessmen and ranchers in their little town in Missouri. It was their fault that the elder Warren couldn't do a day's work. It was their fault that he couldn't always feed his family and his wife had to take in laundry.

Amos came west and homesteaded in Elko County several years before Jack Slater arrived. Much of the land that Jack bought had been on the market, could have been picked up, but Warren's ranch never made enough money for him to buy the land. He couldn't put in a full day's work, had to have help getting into the saddle, and could only hire the least able cow and horse men.

The good ones wouldn't work for the cantanker-ous man and laughed at those who had to help the boss into the saddle. Amos Warren had a hatred for anyone, anything, that showed the air of success. Jack Slater had the temerity to buy the land that Warren was using as grazing land. He dug irriga-tion ditches and brought water to the wrinkled desert, he put up fences and grew fat cows.

Jack Slater brought in a beautiful young woman and married her, had bountiful children, dedi-cated workers. Jack Slater had everything Amos Warren hated. He also had a ranch foreman was more outlaw than cow man and who seemed to have a crew of his own, men who worked more for Sonny Belafleur than Amos Warren. "Never mind," Warren would tell himself. "I get their work and don't have to pay them."

There was a burning desire to get the likes of Jack Slater out of that delightful valley, out of his life. Dead, all of them. Pretty wife, noisy children, and most of all, Jack Slater. Amos Warren ate, drank, worked, and slept with hatred and anger.

6

Jack drove one wagon with Mims and the children on board, while Robbie drove the other with Elizabeth, Cactus Jack, and Two-dog Sorenson riding along. The men all had their saddle horses tied and trailing the wagons. It was about twenty miles into Elko and it didn't take but the first three miles to make some changes.

"I told you it wouldn't work, Jack." Mims was chuckling as she watched all the men getting into one wagon with the women and children in the other. The men had been yelling back and forth about what should and shouldn't be discussed at the meeting the next day and Mims finally demanded the change.

"You were right, my little darlin'," Jack said. "Two-dog drove and the other men got in the back to do their planning. The trip into town was excellent and Mims, with help from Maybell, driving the lead wagon stopped in front of the Cattlemen's Hotel.

"You ladies get us all settled in and we'll get the horses and wagons taken care of," Slater said.

"I know you will and have a snort or two in the saloon, eh?" Elizabeth laughed. "We'll meet you for supper in the dining room in a couple of hours."

"It will be best, Mims, if you ladies and the children went ahead and had supper. I'm more than sure we'll get involved in some discussions about what's going on in the county." Slater gave Mims a hug and a peck on the cheek. "You might even have time for some window shopping before supper."

Mims smiled and gave Elizabeth a big nod. "Yes, there will be," she said.

The saloon at the Cattlemen's Hotel wasn't opulent, as one might expect. Rather it was, maybe because of the trade, rather straight forward. The bar was long, tables were scattered about in the front half while gaming was set up in the back. Mounted deer, antelope and elk heads were lined up along the walls, dominated by a Texas Longhorn on the wall behind the bar.

There were entrances off the bar area to the hotel lobby and the restaurant. It was a busy place, with ranchers, hands, locals and itinerant salesmen lining the long bar. Most of the tables were filled and the gambling tables were busy as well, when Jack brought the crew in.

"The key, here, gentlemen is to listen," he said. "The general meeting will start tomorrow morning, so let's see if we can learn something. Try not to get involved with Amos Warren and his group. It would lead to problems, I'm afraid."

"Might be too late for that, Jack. That's Amos heading straight for us," Cactus Jack said. "It looks like he's put on another fifty pounds or so."

Amos Warren was closing in on forty years and should be in the prime of his life, but suffered from a serious disease known as over-eating, under-working. He owned just a quarter section, one hundred sixty acres, along Huntington Creek, south of Skelton, but ran hundreds of cow-calf pairs every year. He free-ranged his cattle year round, in the Ruby Mountains during the summer months and open prairie in the winter.

"Belafleur is right alongside him, Jack, so make sure I keep my tongue,:" Cactus chuckled. "Just don't like that man."

"Evening, Slater," Warren said. He ignored everyone else in the group. "Here to spout off your nonsense about so-called range management at the meeting tomorrow?"

"As a matter of fact, I am, Amos. After all these years, after all but destroying the range with over use, you still haven't learned a thing, have you? Between the early cattle ranchers and sheep men over using the range, today's management is bringing it back, and operators like you haven't learned a thing."

"Bah! The range is open and free to use, Slater. Limits on use? Stupid, that's what I say. I'll run my cattle anywhere I want. You fence off the open range? I'll tear the fences out."

"You don't want to threaten me like that, Amos Warren. Tear down fences on property I own and you'll pay dearly for it."

"Don't you threaten Mr. Warren," Sonny Belafleur growled. He tried to step between the men but Warren was too rotund for him to get around.

"Mind yourself, Belafleur. It's not your argument," Cactus Jack said. He stood at the bar, his left elbow resting on its top, his right hand close to the big iron at his waist. Ranchers, buckaroos, and others close enough to hear parts of what was being said, slowly backed away. Cactus Jack was a fighter and Sonny Belafleur was known more as a bully. This could blow up instantly.

"It's all right, Cactus." Jack Slater's eyes were narrowed, his mouth was grim, and he was staring hard into Amos Warren's face. "Sonny's just doing what Warren pays him to do. Sonny isn't paid to ramrod a cattle ranch, Cactus. He's paid to intimidate surrounding ranchers into letting Amos's cattle feed on their range."

"Why you," and that's as far as Belafleur got when the barrel of a heavy Colt slammed across the side of his head. His weapon fell to the floor just as his body did and Robbie Slater slipped his Colt back in its holster.

"Don't never pull down on my dad, ever," Robbie said. He bent down and picked up Belafleur's pistol, and laid it on the bar. "Need to teach your men manners, Mr. Warren. Wouldn't hurt to learn some yourself."

Two of Warren's men rushed to the scene, but with Jack, Robbie, Cactus Jack, and Two-dog Sorenson standing there, hands on guns, all they did was drag Sonny Belafleur off to a table. "Be best if you joined them, Amos. I think our conversation is over." Jack Slater had the slightest smile on his face, as he continued, "For now."

"Bah!" Warren moved his hulk back a step or two, turned and made for the dining room, ignoring his bleeding foreman and the men standing around him. Belafleur groaned, coming around, wiped blood from his head, and tried to stand up, couldn't and slumped back into his chair, muttering some foul language.

"Let's take a table gentlemen and see if anyone else wants to have a quiet conversation with us," Slater said, grabbing a bottle of whiskey. "Nice move and appreciated, Rob, but know well, that you just made a big enemy who won't forget."

"I know, Dad, but when he went for his gun I just reacted."

"I'da shot him if I'd seen it," Two-dog said.

"Me, too," Cactus Jack laughed. "He's lucky it was you that saw him, Robbie. Maybe we'll tell him so, next time we meet."

"It's over for the moment," Jack said. "How many others at tomorrow's meeting are going to have the same thoughts as Amos Warren? All the work that's been done since we almost lost the range could be ruined if he has many followers."

"I still think this idea of cutting fences is a smoke screen, giving someone a chance to rustle cattle. There's a market somewhere," Cactus Jack said. "South to Pioche and the railhead down that way is too far, Jack. That would be a five hundred mile drive with stolen cattle. Salt Lake is too far. Reno is too far."

"We know cattle are being rustled, we know brands must be altered, but where would you sell all that prime beef? North to Idaho? It would still be a long drive over rough country, and to a limited market."

"The whole world would see a drive like that," Robbie laughed.

"We're missing something," Slater said. "There's Ted Wilson." Jack waved and his long time friend came over. Wilson ran a three section property north of Elko and was one of the men who helped educate many about range management practices that allowed for continuous use over the years. He often used the word sustainability when he talked about grazing herds of cattle.

"What was that fracas all about, Jack? Hello, Rob. How's married life? You gonna try to beat me roping at the July doings?" He was a jovial man, could be as mean as a wolf and was a true horseman, raising some of the finest stock in eastern Nevada.

"Nice to see you, Ted," Jack said. "Sonny Belafleur pulled down on me and Rob took care of the problem. Any problems up north here? Got some fence cutters down south. Four of 'em hit Wes Trimble's place. One's still alive, but none of them are known. Tried to run off with about a hundred of his beef."

"Got some cattle gone missing, fences down, and a few stupid people running around," Wilson laughed.

"If you came up with a couple of hundred head of cattle with mixed brands and you had no morals, where would you sell them?" Jack asked. "Reports of missing cattle from all over the county, Ted, but I'll be if I can figure out where they would be sold."

"One of the ideas I'm bringing up at our meeting tomorrow, Jack, might just answer your question. I'm going to suggest that we form a group called Range Riders, whose only purpose will be to watch over the open range in the county."

"How, so?" Cactus Jack asked. "To what purpose?"

"Two main reasons," Wilson said. "Keep track of how many cattle are out there and two, watch for large herds of cattle being moved. Those stealing cattle have to move them somewhere and quickly after taking them."

"Pretty big order," Rob said. "Who's gonna pay these Range Riders, Ted?"

"So that's why the Slater place is so successful, eh Jack? Someone watching the purse? Good question, Rob. I'm proposing that members of the organization contribute to the fund. Only have to find a few hundred stolen cows to pay for something like this."

"You can guarantee a no vote from Amos Warren," Jack laughed. "You're thinking something that you haven't come right out and said, Ted. Gonna give us a hint?"

"The western Nevada market is large, despite all the ranches in the Truckee Meadows and Carson Valley. The northern California market is huge, despite all the ranches there. What if you didn't have to drive stolen cattle?" He had a smile on his face, got up, nodded to everyone, and made his way to the bar.

"Most interesting," Slater said. "He's implying railroads, but cattle are strictly checked for proper branding and ownership before hauling. Might need to think on that, Rob, Cactus. Let's eat."

Rob Slater couldn't get Ted Wilson's comment out of his head. *What did he mean by that? He said, what if you didn't have to drive stolen cattle in order to get them to the large market areas. Can't put them on rail cars without proper paperwork and in today's world, that means fully legal and proven ownership.*

"Not the best night I've ever had," Robbie said. He was walking down to breakfast with Elizabeth. "We'll be in these meetings all day, Liz and I'm gonna need some serious tender, long, sweet hours with you tonight. To get me over it all, you understand."

"You're funny, Rob. You talked in your sleep half the night. What are you upset about?"

"Moving cattle long distances without driving them or using the railroad. My puzzle for the day."

"Good luck," she chuckled. "Teach 'em to fly, Rob."

7

The general meeting of the Elko County Cattlemen was rowdy, fun, and educational, according to Rob Slater. Jack left out the fun part, as did Cactus Jack. Two-dog Sorenson slept through most of it. "My head hurts," Rob said. "Old man Warren made a fool of himself, demanding that the organization ask the governor to grant ownership to whoever puts his cattle on open range."

"Maybe," Jack said. "The man had others who agreed with him. Not many, but there are those who want without the means of having. Ted Wilson's idea might gain some sympathy, though. Be a way to know more about how the range is used. Sometimes we forget that others use the range, too."

"Who?" Cactus asked.

"The wild animals and birds were there first. There are those who were here earlier and remember how large the herds of deer and antelope were." Jack said.

"No more words until half a gallon of beer has passed these parched lips," Cactus Jack said. "It was only during that wonderful mid-day dinner that people quit talking. Roasted spring lamb tends to do that to folk."

"Ate a pound of pickled tongue, myself," Two-dog Sorenson said. "I liked that Basque lady who made it, too. Gonna dance with her at the party tonight. We already talked about that."

"Well, will you listen to our own Lothario," Jack Slater said. "Good for you, Two-dog."

"That just ain't right, Two-dog. I do believe you also promised young Jenifer Trimble a dance or two." Cactus Jack wasn't going to let up on Two-dog either. "Man of your stature can't be sashaying around with two women, and at your age, too."

"I'm gonna whup on you, Cactus Jack Faraday," Two-dog said, but the laughter from Rob, Jack, and Cactus Jack held him in check. "Jennifer brought several of her knives, Cactus, and I'm gonna tell her to charge you double." He got a big smile. "Or maybe just use one of them. We're giving each other knives at supper tonight, so you'd best hold it in, Cactus Jack Faraday."

Even Two-dog couldn't hold in the laughter when Cactus feigned a wild right and Two-dog ducked away. The saloon in the Cattlemen's was filling fast, everyone talking at the same time, enjoying cold beer, platters of sliced cold meats, and locally made cheeses. "I'm going to make sure Mims has found someone to sit with the children. She has been looking forward to this party tonight for a long time." Jack Slater walked toward the hotel lobby, saying hello to many, having a hard time getting away from some.

"Won't see him until the party," Rob said. "Let's stand at the bar. I've been sitting in hard chairs all day. Have you given any more thought to what Ted Wilson was talking about? Moving cattle hundreds of miles without driving them or freighting them?"

"Yup, and I think the man's lost a shoe nail." Two-dog said. "Horse shoe's gonna fall right off soon. Can't do what he says." Cactus Jack was laughing at the comment, but Two-dog kept right on. "Four hundred miles to Reno and ain't no way of moving them critters 'ceptin' what we knows."

He wanted to say more but the laughter from the others slowed him down enough that he took a minute to look around. "Watch out," he bellowed as a chair came flying at them. It was followed by Sonny Belafleur and two Warren buckaroos. Belafleur's head was partially covered by a bloody bandage and he aimed his charge right at Rob Slater.

"You're gonna die, boy," he cried. His lunge was shunted quickly by the sidestepping Slater who drove a fist into Belafleur's side. He followed by twisting and getting away from the bar. Belafleur lunged again and the two crashed onto a table, taking it to the floor in splinters. Rob was on his back and slammed his two open hands together with Belafleur's head in between, rolled hard and jumped to his feet.

A boot to the Warren brand's foreman ended the fracas and again, Sonny Belafleur had to be helped to a chair. Cactus Jack had a choke hold on one buckaroo, pulled his pistol and knocked the man out, while Two-dog Sorenson did a three-punch series on the other. Two-dog reached for the knife on his belt and Cactus stopped him.

"You come messing with the Slater brand again, Belafleur and I'll gut shoot you," Rob said. "You got the manners of a muck rootin' hog, Belafleur. You stay away from me and the Slater ranch."

He was leaning into Belafleur's face, screaming at him, wanting to shoot him twice over, and Cactus Jack eased him away. "Good job, Rob. Now, let the man enjoy his aches and pains. Let's have a cold beer." The crowd parted quickly as he led the three to a table and motioned for pitchers of beer.

A deputy sheriff walked up to the table. "You all right, Slater? Want to press charges? I watched the whole thing."

"I think he did press charges," Two-dog laughed.

"No, I don't think that would be necessary. He's hurtin' enough for now, but if you find me back-shot in the next few weeks, you better have a long rope for him." Rob smiled and grabbed a glass of beer and drained it that fast. "That man's a fool."

The deputy nodded and walked back to the bar. "You're right," Cactus said. "And the man he works for is a bigger fool. How much you want to bet they're gonna want to charge the Slaters for that wrecked table?"

Robbie laughed through bruised ribs and nodded his agreement. "Jack'll love that."

"That boy needs killin'." Sonny Belafleur groaned as he tried to sit up straight. He took a pull on the whiskey bottle and groaned again.

"I got a better way of gettin' him," Toby Forbes said. "Ever looked at that sweet little girl that boy's married up to? Something should happen to her would hurt that boy bad."

"Bring the whole Slater ranch down on you," Belafleur snarled. He sat still, took another long drink of whiskey, this time from a glass and smiled. "On the other hand, you might have the answer, Toby. I wasn't gonna go to that dance tonight, but I might just have to. You gentlemen know how to dance?"

Forbes, nodded and Owen 'Three-toes' Jacobs laughed. "I can dance," Toby said, "But old Three-toes here might have a problem with that."

"No, no," Jacobs said. "I can dance just fine. You shove a pretty girl into these arms, and I'm a dancin' fool."

"Listen to what I was just thinkin', then." Sonny Belafleur spent the next ten minutes lining out how they would create Liz Slater's worst night ever.

There was a long spring sunset sprinkling colors everywhere in the western skies as several hundred people gathered at the Elko County Fairgrounds for the annual Elko County Cattlemen's dinner and dance. Great roasts of beef, lamb, and pork were sizzling over hot coals and cauldrons of beans were bubbling wonderful aromas into the brisk evening air. This was a buckaroo festival and all the talk was horses, cattle, and more horses.

Those with musical instruments were tuning up, or just playing favorites. Mims and Elizabeth were in their finest, Jack and the other men were showing off their best hats, vests, and frock coats and talk of beef, weather, range, and price filtered through the air. The music would follow platters of meat, along with pies and ice cream. It was the social event of the year in eastern Nevada.

"Got lucky on the weather this year," Ted Wilson said, joining the Slater table. "We've feasted in the rain before, eh Jack?"

"And snow and mud and whatever else the old man up there could throw at us. Think you can get that Range Rider idea of yours through the legislature? Have the state pay for it? I'd be more inclined to keep it local and we, that is, us ranchers, pay for it."

"I'm sure that's how it'll play out, Jack. Suggesting it should be at the state level will get many upset and they'll take the alternative."

"You're a devious devil, Mr. Wilson," Liz laughed. "That's how you got me to be your housekeeper before I married Rob." She looked around the table. "He gave me alternatives, as I remember. Go to an orphan's home in Reno or be his housekeeper. Not much of an alternative," she laughed.

"I talked with the sheriff a few minutes ago," Ted Wilson continued, trying to ignore the comment. "The two dead rustlers and the wounded one aren't known by anyone here and what paper he could find is from Colorado. Two-bit gamblers and con men. It isn't logical that four men would show up out of nowhere and start rustling cattle in Elko County."

"No way of knowing if those four are also the ones taking cattle in other parts of the county," Jack Slater said. "Might be a gang that's moved in."

"I'm gonna ask again," Rob said. "How do we move stolen cattle to large markets, Ted, without driving them or using the railroad? I've been working on your comment since you made it. Must be a trick question."

"Not at all, Rob. Not at all," Wilson said. "Cut 'em up and move 'em in boxes." He sat back with a 'gotcha' look spread across his face. "Railroad's been using refrigerated cars for years, Rob. There is one packing house right next to the feedlots operating that way, right here in Elko. Course they wouldn't deal in stolen beef, but do we know if there is another? Or more? If someone is moving cattle quickly to feedlots attached to a packing house, then cut up beef could be moved to any market the railroad serves."

"Take a pretty good chunk of money to set something like that up, Ted." Jack Slater had an amazed look as he glanced up and down the table. "A hidden feedlot, packing house, and access to the railroad?"

"It would take a lot of money and effort, but the return would be excellent. The operation would either have to be clandestine or appear completely legal, to pull it off. It would certainly answer the question of vanishing herds of cattle."

"Let's ease away from this conversation, Ted. It looks like Amos Warren is heading this way. I'm wondering how much he knows about his foreman's activities? Or, if he directs those movements."

"He isn't gonna like what happened this afternoon," Rob chuckled. "maybe we should call Two-dog over. He's sitting with Jennifer Trimble's family, comparing knives. He was about to carve Sonny Belafleur into tiny pieces this afternoon."

8

"Evening, Wilson, Slater." Amos Warren was an angry man and his two hundred fifty pounds were aching for a fight. "You." He growled it out, pointed a fat finger at Robbie. "You dirty little Mex, you ever attack one of my men again and I'll have you strung up high."

What is it that would cause a man to say such a thing? Warren hated Jack Slater, and may have had angry thoughts about young Slater beating the tar out of his foreman, but why the slur? Ignorance? Most in the valley were well aware of Robbie's background, his no-good father, a Spanish diplomat who ran away from his responsibilities. Certainly not a Mexican and what if he was? Something was very wrong with Amos Warren.

Jack Slater swung his right fist as he was jumping to his feet, burying it Warren's jowly jaw, knocking the man ten feet back and flat on his back. There was nothing more important to Jack Slater than his family and Rob was his adopted son, a son in every aspect of the word. "How dare you," Slater said, so softly only Mims heard him.

Slater lost his family when he was ten, Mims lost hers earlier and the two met after being placed in a home in Dakota Territory. The man grew up hard, but with a personal set of ethics that simply would not bend and challenging his family would not be tolerated.

Ted Wilson grabbed Robbie and held him. "No, son, this isn't your fight. At least for the moment, it isn't. It's Jack's fight, Rob and you'll see how decent men hold their family. Just watch."

Robbie Slater had faced this before. Before he was a Slater, even as a child and it seemed it would never go away. *I'm not a Mexican, and even if I was, I'm sure that my reaction would be the same. Half Spanish is what I am and I'm proud of that. If I was Mexican, I'd be proud of that, too.* Robbie's mind was trying to sort out all the feelings ripping through his system. *I love Jack and Mims, proud of being their son. Why would Amos Warren say something like that?* He tried to ease up, to relax, as Wilson had asked, but it wasn't easy.

Jack stood over Amos Warren's walrus body, reached down and slapped him, open handed, across the face. "Apologize, Mr. Warren." He didn't yell it out, didn't hold a fist in the man's face, just spoke the words, softly. It was the most embarrassing thing a man could do to another man. Open handed slap, in front of his own men, and Amos Warren just lay there, taking it.

The slap was so loud that even those who hadn't seen or heard Warren going down, looked around. The second slap resounded through the large fairgrounds show-building and men were ready to start putting money on the outcome. Amos Warren had been baiting Jack Slater for two days, had set his foreman on attack mode, and Slater, apparently, had all he would take.

Men were moving their families back and away from the fray, others were feeling about their frock coats and dress wear to make sure they were fully armed. Only a few of the women cried out, children tried to get closer, to see what the fuss was. The cooks continued basting the huge roasts on their rotisseries.

"No one talks to my family that way, Mr. Warren. Apologize in three seconds. One, two, three." And this time it was a hard, left fist, straight out of the shoulder into the middle of Warren't face. The cattleman's nose exploded in a shower of blood and a squeal of pain. He was probably unconscious when the second fist drove into the groove between his eyes. He had not apologized.

It was Sheriff Mossie Peabody who pulled Jack Slater back from the unconscious body. "That's enough, Jack. You've made your point." Peabody said it loud enough for many to hear, but most didn't see Sonny Belafleur come running, his revolver in hand. Toby Forbes and Odie Jackson right behind.

"Look out," Robbie bawled. He wrenched free of Ted Wilson, drawing his sidearm, and took a quick shot, knocking Belafleur to the ground. Peabody whirled around in time to take a bullet through his leg from Jackson and Jack Slater killed Toby Forbes with two quick shots. There was bedlam inside the great fairgrounds show-building as women and children were hustled out, men grabbed heavy iron but didn't know who to shoot and the rush for the doors was a stampede.

Odie Jackson turned and ran hard for the doors and Two-dog Sorenson started to give chase, but the crowd was too much to fight through. "That was Odie Jackson got away," he yelled out. Rob raced to where Jack was tending Mossie Peabody's wound just as Amos Warren started coming around. He saw Sonny Belafleur crawling toward Jack, blood staining his left leg.

He had his Colt aimed at Belafleur's right eye. "Far enough," he said. He kicked the revolver out of the wounded man's hands and whacked him across the side of his already bleeding head.

Two-dog helped get Belafleur into a chair next to Warren. Peabody was sitting on the other side of Warren, all three bleeding hard.

Skelton deputy Rick Burdick ran over. "Go get a doc, Ricky," Peabody said. "None of us are gonna die but we do need help. Get a couple of deputies in here, too. They should be close-by." The sheriff looked at Jack Slater with just a half grin on his face. "Don't suppose you'd like to tell me what started this little dance, would you?"

"I know why I smashed Warren's face in, Sheriff, but this has been building for some time and you know it. Cut fences, rustled herds. It's like the 1870s again, not almost the twentieth century. We're supposed to be civilized." Mossie Peabody tried his best to hold back a chuckle.

"Burdick said those outlaws that hit Trimble's place cut the fence late at night. One had a note on him that simply said, 'see you in Elko,' or something like that. Have you had any fences cut?"

"No, but it's been threatened by Sonny, there. My men keep pretty close track of things, but I'd put a lot of money on Belafleur being involved some way or another." Slater wondered if Sonny Belafleur worked for Amos Warren or was it the other way around? What if Belafleur was using Warren and all his nonsense about open range and fences to run a rustling gang?

"Harsh words, Slater, but I will take them under advisement. I guess you heard, the men from Trimbles' place were from Colorado. No known connections around Elko County."

Burdick came back with three deputies and the doctor. "Get Forbes' body out of here, take Mr. Belafleur into custody and Doc, see if you can get us patched up enough to move." The sheriff was still the sheriff, despite his wounds. "Get some calm around here and let these people enjoy their party."

The deputies dispersed, spreading the word that it was all over, safe now to enjoy your dinner and dance. Mossie Peabody wasn't sure it was all over, but at least it was for the time being.

Odie Jackson made it to his horse and rode hard for the little camp Sonny Belafleur had set up for the Warren ranch hands. "Toby's dead, and Sonny's been shot." He called it out as he jumped from his horse. "Jack Slater attacked Mr. Warren and he might be hurt bad, too. We gotta do something."

"You sure about Toby?" Thomas Forbes, called Skinny by most, asked. He was Toby's older brother. "Who did it? Tell me now, Odie. Who did it?" The anger flushed his face, his eyes were narrowed to slits and he would kill anyone at that moment.

"It was the Mex kid, calls himself Rob Slater. The one that beat up Sonny yesterday. He's gonna die if I have anything to say about it."

"You better not get in my way, Odie. I'm the one killing that kid," Skinny Forbes said. "Where's Sonny? Why ain't he with you?"

"Like I said, Sheriff's got him. He was shot in the leg, I think. The whole Slater ranch was looking to kill us as soon as we showed up. Me, Forbes, and Sonny were gonna have fun with that Slater kid's new wife. Maybe they heard about that."

Skinny Forbes stood by the fire, looking around at the Warren buckaroos. He and Odie worked for Sonny Belafleur, but not these others. They were simply ranch hands called on from time to time to help move other people's cattle. Now, with Toby dead and Sonny wounded and probably in jail, they were seriously short-handed.

"We lost those three Colorado men, Odie, lost Trimble's herd, too, and now lost old Toby and Sonny. Ride out to the plant and let them know what's going on. Have to make some changes around here right away. You can be there by sunrise."

Odie Jackson was the oldest of the outlaw gang, walked with a limp from time to time, the results of a forty five from up close and personal. He was a knife man and let his opponent get back and shoot him. "Let me grab a quick bite and some whiskey," he said. He cut off a slab of meat being roasted and grabbed a bottle. He was back on his horse in less than five minutes.

Skinny Forbes stood by the fire, watched Odie ride out, and wondered what else could possibly go wrong. *The perfect deal. Steal 'em, slaughter 'em, package 'em, and ship 'em out. Maybe all gone now. Maybe time for me to be all gone, too. Sure as all get-out somebody's gonna get wise to this operation. It was wrong for Belafleur to be leading. Man can't think.*

Losing the Trimble cattle was a blow. Blake Wilson had been running the Halleck Feed Lot for three years and just recently built the adjoining packing house facilities. Wilson had been a cattle broker in Denver before moving to Nevada, at the urgent request of the Denver police department. His feedlot wasn't always that much interested in proper branding and ownership, and now, with the packing house, he could even be more liberal when it came to ownership of what he bought.

He was clever, building the packing house, bringing in a partner who didn't exist. The new packing house owner was listed as Willard Covington, a millionaire recluse from San Francisco. Wilson was named general manager and was allowed to sign all legal documents regarding the plant. No one had questioned the deal. *I don't know why Belafleur wasn't with those Denver men I brought in to help move cattle. He was supposed to be using cow men not those men I brought in. They were just extra guns.*

All the modern facilities were in place at the packing plant, including the freezing and refrigeration of carcasses and boxed sections. The railroad had a spur for the feed lot already, so a quick extension allowed for refrigerated cars to come right up to the loading docks. Blake Wilson found Sonny Belafleur a stupid but willing partner in the scheme. He was remembering when they put it all together.

"You have a quick temper, Belafleur," Wilson said to the man when they made their deal. "It had best not get us in trouble. You bring me fine cattle and I'll do all the rest. No one but you and Odie Jackson are to be aware of our deal. Don't let your big gun and fast fists destroy what I've built here."

It was later that the Forbes brothers were brought in. They had connections in Colorado and New Mexico Territory. Skinny Forbes quickly became one of Blake Wilson's favorite men to work with.

Belafleur stuck to his deal. He and Jackson put together a group of rowdy outlaws and rustled cattle all over Elko County, funneling them to the Wilson Feedlot. It was a lucrative operation. Bills of sale were always on hand if someone dared to ask, ranchers were aware that they had missing cattle, but they were generally taken from downed fences and how the fences were downed was questionable. Missing cattle or rustled cattle? Call the sheriff or not? Where were the cattle? Searches across the open prairie didn't find any and none showed up at markets, either.

One big mistake was taking, not ten or twenty head, but one hundred or more from Wes Trimble and then having Trimble kill the rustlers and regain his herd. This was a thorn beginning to fester in Wilson's mind.

Wilson's plan came from an idea he tried in Denver but without the help of a feed lot. Because of the feed lot, all the cattle that went to the packing house had already been cleared by way of brands and bills of sale. The product being shipped from the packing house didn't need further inspection. Running brands altered whatever was brought in to fit whatever the bills of sale said. Eyebrows had been raised a time or two, but nothing ever was followed through.

A branding law was enacted in 1873 but there were no state brand inspectors. The brands were registered with individual county recorders. If cattle came to the feedlot with brands matching those on the bills of sale, everything stopped right there. Wilson had himself a goldmine.

"Belafleur's getting sloppy, Mr. Jackson. Losing a herd of fine cattle? Getting shot and tossed in the slammer? Losing a man? This operation of mine is dependent on suppliers being able to operate and something like this could bring the sheriff and district attorney down on us in a flash."

Odie Jackson was bone tired, didn't need a tongue lashing from some dude from Denver who deals in stolen product. "I'll see to it he knows how you feel, Wilson. You got something else on your mind? If not, I'm gonna find my bedroll somewhere comfortable."

"You can sleep in the saddle, Jackson. I want you and Skinny Forbes back here this evening. Changes are going to be made and I mean soon. No back talk, Jackson. Get on that horse and ride out now."

The older man wanted to shoot Wilson in the stomach, twice, but slowly got himself settled in the saddle and rode back toward Elko. Wilson reached out and swatted the horse, and chuckled, watching Jackson have to grab the saddle horn. *He'll stop as soon as he's out of sight and grab some sleep. That's the least of my problems right now. I need a new supplier and soon. Skinny Forbes is more capable than Belafleur, but I wonder if he can find people to ride with him? Belafleur will have to be eliminated and soon. With his temper, a shove or two in painful places and he'll tell everything he knows.*

9

"We need to get back to the ranch as soon as possible, Mims. Andy Pettigrew is a good hand, but the only people with him are a couple of buckaroos. Amos Warren ain't gonna take my beating lightly. We'll leave out right after an early breakfast. Make sure Wanda has the children ready."

"You need to talk to Robbie, Jack. He's hurting bad by what Amos Warren said. We treat him as if he's a full grown man, Jack, but he's still a boy. A married boy, the boy cow-boss of the Slater Ranch," she chuckled. "But too aware of his background. His is different from ours, you know."

Mims was always aware of their backgrounds. She and Jack, orphans, but different. He lost his parents in a tragic accident, she never knew hers. Mims had no idea of who she came from, what they may have been like, and, now, Robbie. "He had to watch his mother die from that terrible infection and knew what a miserable man his father was. He has to be fragile right now, Jack. We need to be as close as we can be."

"I know, Mims, and I forget that often, I guess. He's my son is all I ever think about. Sometimes my mind reels back in time and I can still see you coming out of Jablonski's kitchen door, glowing with life. You kept me in line, you know. I would have hurt that old man if it hadn't been for you." He took Mims in his arms and planted a smack on her lips.

"It's a real shame that Rob's father was such a foul man. A Spanish diplomat? No," Jack said. "A philanderer and never a father. Robbie's with Ted Wilson right now, so I'll join them. You and Liz head back to the hotel. We'll be along. I'll make this up to you."

"Just being Jack Slater is enough for me."

He stood and watched Mims gather up Elizabeth and Two-dog for the ride back to the hotel and ambled over to where Ted Wilson and Robbie were talking. "Guess I just about ruined the Cattlemen's great party for this year, eh Ted?"

"What you ruined was Amos Warren's nose, Jack. The walking wounded are being taken care of. Let's you, Rob, and I have a little discussion, shall we? I've got a flask of Horseface Hawkins' finest." They walked to one of the tables, still set for the supper and took chairs. "Looks like many are staying, Jack and there's still plenty of food."

"I guess I won't get a bill from the cattlemen for uneaten grub." Jack was chuckling as he took his seat, nodded to several seated at tables nearby. Several men gave him a thumb's up gesture and several women were seen scowling.

"Rob, we need to have another one of those talks neither one of us likes," Jack Slater said.

"I know, Dad. I don't like it when people talk to me like that."

"I guess you noticed, I don't either." Jack said.

Hearty laughter erupted from all three men and Wilson pulled the flask from his inside coat pocket. "Definitely time for a drink," Wilson said. "I wouldn't put too much into what an ignorant man says, Rob."

"I know, Mr. Wilson, but I even got that talk from some of the professors at the university when I was in Reno last year. It hurts," he said. "I can throw a steer, whip just about anyone, but those kinds of ugly words hurt."

"Schooling doesn't cure certain types of ignorance, Rob." Wilson watched Rob's arms flex, watched his fists getting balled, saw jaw muscles tighten, and was thankful he wouldn't be facing the young man's anger. "One can't argue with an ignorant man, Rob, because the ignorant man will demand to be accepted as not ignorant. Therefore what he says, how he feels, will always be right in his mind. Best philosophy? Ignore the ignorant."

"Might be easier said than done, Rob," Jack said. "It is the best thing to do, though. You're far more intelligent than most. Use that against them, not rage, not violence. Shame them, Rob and walk away. That's something I don't always follow."

Jack sat back, looking deep into his son's big brown eyes and wondered about himself. *I certainly didn't take my own advice, beating the tar out of old Amos.* Jack almost chuckled at the thought. "You're the legitimate son of a Spanish diplomat who wasn't up to being a father and of a wonderful mother who died far too young. You're Mims' and my son, Rob. You have a heart as big as the sky and friends by the score. Those like Amos Warren are beneath you in so many ways. Don't let them grow."

The flask was passed around the table again and Ted Wilson tucked it back inside his jacket. "Good words, good bourbon, good friends. Let's call it a night, eh?"

Rob knew they were right, but there was a burning desire to stomp Amos Warren, shoot him twice, and burn the remains. "I know stupid people believe their own stupidity, Dad. I've had to work with some and I've watched you work with some. I'd just really like to get even sometimes."

"Some call it retribution, son. Some call it revenge. In the end, many call it bitter."

"That's all I know, Skinny. Wilson said to bring you to the packing plant pronto. He's one angry man right now." Odie Jackson had taken a four hour sleep along the trail and it was late in the day when he arrived at the Warren camp site outside Elko. "Have you seen Amos Warren or Sonny?"

"Warren took a beating, if his face is some indication and is riding back to the ranch. Wants us all back right away. Sonny took a bullet to his leg and almost bled to death. He's chained to his bed in the hospital and will be in jail when he heals. You gotta know how angry that wolf is right now."

"He's not alone," Jackson said. "Wilson talks down to me just a couple more times and he'll find one of my knives deep in his belly. Tired of being talked down to, Skinny. Tired of it." Odie Jackson was never a good buckaroo and didn't last a season at the few ranches he signed with. His temper flashed at inopportune times leading to jail, injury, subjection. In his current state, he would kill first before thinking.

Forbes sent the Warren buckaroos back to the ranch then he and Jackson rode out to the feedlot near Halleck. "What are we riding into, Jackson? I don't much care for Wilson, either, but I sure do admire his operation. We can plunder the Skelton range, the Ruby Valley, the areas north of Elko with ease. What we need to do is separate from Amos Warren. This close association without

Warren knowing what we're doing is going to come back on us hard."

"It was Sonny's idea to use Warren as our reason for being around. He called Warren a blind. It wasn't Blake Wilson's idea, Skinny. Might want to bring it up to Wilson."

"I told Skunk not to take the entire Trimble herd, but oh, no, he said Sonny wanted the entire herd at one time. Got hisself kilt, it did. Easy to move ten or so head quickly to the feedlot, running through the night like we've been doing. But running off with the whole herd? Hard to manage, hard to move 'em fast. Stupid and he paid for it."

The plan was easy. Break down a fence and let the herd scatter out. Pick ten or fifteen good looking steers and run them to the feedlot. By the time the rancher has found and gathered his herd they would be long gone when the rancher discovers missing cattle.

"Yeah, he was stupid. Are we? We don't have much of a crew, Skinny. We need to find people or get out. Sure as all get out, some lawman's gonna get interested."

It was dark when they rode into the feedlot and got their horses put up. "Evening, Wilson. Looks like Sonny Belafleur will be out of the picture for a while."

"For a long while, Mr. Forbes. A forever long while." Blake Wilson had an ugly look on his face, a mangled cigar shoved in his mouth, and a glass of whiskey in his hand. "Come in, I was just getting ready for supper." He stepped aside and Jackson and Forbes walked into a spacious ranch house that doubled as the feedlot offices. "Ling Ho, prepare two more suppers, please. We have guests."

The Chinese cook bowed and scurried back into the kitchen. "Let's sit by the fire and talk business before supper. Whiskey?" Wilson asked. A huge rock fireplace dominated one wall of the rough beamed room and featured the mounted head of a magnificent Texas longhorn. Other game animal mounts were scattered around the various walls. Braided throw rugs covered hardwood floors and Tiffany lamps added a warm glow to the vast room. In a stand near the front door was an array of rifles and shotguns within easy reach.

"I'm making some big changes effective this instant, gentlemen. Sonny Belafleur needs to be eliminated. Do we hire the job or do it ourselves?"

"Ourselves meaning me or Odie?" Skinny Forbes looked Wilson directly in the eye. "Hanging for murder hurts just as much as hanging for rustling, I guess. Ain't no crew left, Mr. Wilson. Got some ideas on how this should be done?" Forbes had been around a long time, served time in Carson City, Huntsville. and other equally horrible prisons. Money is what separated the various crimes, not how the public might rank them. "Cost might factor into this plan, too."

Wilson couldn't hold back his grin and saw a sly grin spread across Odie Jackson's face as well. "I'm sure it will," Wilson said. "One of the changes I'm making is not bringing in outside help unless they will also become part of our operation. The Warren thing that Belafleur insisted on was wrong. Where, exactly, is Belafleur?"

"He's chained to his bed in the hospital until his leg heals. Then it's off to jail," Odie said.

"Easier to get him there than in jail, eh?" Wilson said. Ling Ho called out that supper was ready and the men moved to the oak table that sat ten comfortably. The three men gathered at one end to continue their conversation.

"If Sheriff Peabody is allowing visitors I'll go see him." Skinny Forbes wanted the job. He was certain that it was Sonny who caused his brother's death. "Otherwise, it might actually be easier in jail. Do something dumb, get thrown in the hoosegow for a day, and do the deed. Lots of witnesses, but I already got paper out on me anyway," he laughed.

"Bring the whole county down on us, Skinny. Do it at the hospital, quick, clean, even if you aren't allowed in as a visitor. No witnesses. In fact, don't try to be a visitor, sneak in, unseen."

Supper was a spring lamb that once belonged

to a nearby rancher and the brandy afterward made conversation pleasant. "Now, other changes. Break away from Warren. His mouth and attitude will surely lead someone to these doors. We have a shortage of men right now, also. About seven short before yesterday, I think. Can't move cattle without men, and they have to be cleared by me before too much is said to them."

"I understand, Wilson," Odie Jackson said. "There's a couple of fellows I know who might want a good job. I'll bring 'em around."

"Good. I sent wires to Denver, too. We have to save this operation, it's just too good to lose." The operation could move from fifty to one hundred head a month without raising alarms. The boxed and frozen beef could go in any direction. Where ever the current buyers were and the markets were open year around.

"Throw your bedrolls out in front of the fire, boys. We'll talk more in the morning. Skinny, consider yourself the lead man."

10

"Slater's gonna pay for this," Amos Warren said. He was in his bedroom glaring into a mirror reflecting his mashed nose, black eyes, and split lip. He had a raging headache, his bowels were acting up, and he wanted to see blood flowing in every direction from the Slater ranch.

Owen Jacobs, called three-toes from a birth defect, knocked on the bedroom door. "Got a pot of coffee, Mr. Warren."

"Put some brandy in it, Three-toes and call a meeting. I'll meet with the crew in the barn in fifteen minutes. I want everyone there."

Three-toes left the pot and a bottle then hustled out to the corrals where the Warren buckaroos were gathered for their morning talk. Belafleur would normally be assigning duties, but without the foreman, everyone was just standing around, spittin' and chewin'.

"Warren wants everyone in the barn in fifteen minutes." Three-toes looked around. "Where's Odie and Skinny?"

"Didn't ride back with us," Jake Winters piped up. "We're missing others, too. What's going on, Three-toes?"

"Don't know. Warren's face took a fall off a cliff somewhere, Sonny's in jail, Toby's dead, and those four new riders, I don't know, just disappeared."

"I don't much care for riding for this brand," Willard Austin said. "Helping to move cattle that don't have Warren's brand on 'em? Men riding off on personal jobs? Foreman going to jail? Ain't no place for a cow man."

"Well, let's see what Warren has in mind," Three-toes said. The men, talking among themselves, ambled from the corrals to the barn. It was just a few minutes and Amos Warren came trudging across the yard. His weight and sedentary life made it difficult for him to walk with any kind of purposeful stride.

"Good mornin', men." Those standing closest almost had to turn away to keep their grins and snickers hidden and those in the back tried to see more of the man's pudgy and well-worn face. "We're facing the prospect of a range war, I'm afraid. Open war between the Warren brand and the outlaw Slater ranch. I was severely beaten by

Jack Slater last night, he killed Toby Forbes, and shot Sonny Belafleur."

Three-toes Jacobs sucked in a deep breath, remembering how the play went down and it certainly didn't go the way Warren just described it. He looked around and realized that none of the men had been there. Odie Jackson was there, but he's not here. Warren looked at Wilson. "Where are Odie Jackson and Skinny Forbes?"

"Didn't ride back with us, Boss. Maybe taking care of Skinny's brother's body."

"I want to see them as soon as they get back. Winters, I want you and Austin to ride into Skelton and find out just how many men that outlaw Jack Slater has on his place? We're gonna burn that man out." Anger flared when the men didn't respond immediately. "Ride out now, don't just stand around pickin' your nose."

Jake Winters and Willard Austin had their horses already saddled, set for the day's work, and rode out toward Skelton at a lope. "What did he mean, we're gonna burn Slater out?" Willard Austin asked. They only had seven or eight miles to ride and Austin wasn't the kind of cow man who burned out neighbors. "Is he crazy?"

"Slater sure isn't an outlaw," Winters said. "Must have been quite a brawl last night. Wish we'd been there."

"I ain't ridin' for no brand that burns out neighbors," Austin said. "Wish we'd had time to talk to Three-toes about this. He had a pained look on his face when Warren talked about burning Slater out."

"I saw that, too. I guess the best place to find out about Slater's place would be the Alabama House Saloon, eh, Mr. Austin?"

"I need a good taste of good whiskey after this morning," Austin laughed. Austin came to Nevada after a long drive from west Texas to Kansas, looking for new excitements. He was raised on the open ranges of Texas, had more cow sense than most, and loyalty to your brand was all but burned into his hip. *I ain't gonna do what Mr. Warren wants. I ain't gonna burn out a neighbor. Jake can turn in my time and grab whatever money I got coming. This is as far as I go.*

Jack Slater met Cactus Jack and Robbie at the hotel dining room table for an early morning talk while the women got the children ready for the ride home. "That was a real mess last night, gentlemen. Cactus, I want you and Rob to take the men, including Two-dog, back to the ranch and do a fence check. Don't be slow about it, either. Amos Warren threw down the gauntlet last night when he threatened to burn us out, and he ain't gonna not follow through. "I'll send Mims, Liz, and the kids straight home and ride to Skelton to have a talk with Skelton Deputy Burdick."

"You think they'll be safe? Alone like that? I'd sure feel better if Two-dog Sorenson rode with them. Dad. That's a long twenty miles and who knows what Warren might already have planned."

"I guess you're right. Let Two-dog ride with the women and children. I'm off," Jack said.

"And a wee sip at the Alabama House?" Cactus Jack called out. "Let's get 'em rolling, Rob. We can burn off some of our anger on the ride back. You beat the dickens out of Belafleur and it was supposed to be my chore, not yours. I got one coming now."

"You take two men and ride the home sections, Cactus and I'll take two and ride the new one, that now carries my brand. Glad to get out of this town. Me and Mister Belafleur had a go at it, Cactus, but it's Mr. Warren who's gonna find out just how tough this Slater is. Ain't nobody ever gonna talk to me that way again, and ain't nobody gonna burn out the Slater family."

Jack chuckled watching the two joust with each other heading for the stables and their horses. Jack finished his coffee and found Mims, Liz, and the children ready to leave. "I'll get the teams harnessed. Liz, you drive one wagon with Maybelle assisting and Mims the other with Seth and little Jack. Two-dog will ride along on his horse. Don't expect anything, but Warren's a strange man at best." He took a quick kiss from Mims and let the frown lift from his craggy face. "If you ladies don't mind, I'm going to ride on ahead. I need to spread the word in Skelton about those threats that Amos Warren made. You're more than safe today, I'm sure."

"We'll be fine Jack. Liz has a scatter gun and Seth says he can take on anyone." She giggled, flirted with Jack right out. "Hurry home. We'll have it warm for you," Mims said. They watched him ride off at a lope and got everyone loaded up for the twenty mile ride. "Might have to stop at the springs for a little picnic, Liz. Can't waste a beautiful spring morning like this. What do you say to that, Two-dog?"

"If you have a wee bit of apple pie, it might just make a fine day for a picnic," he laughed.

Jack tied off in front of Valley Paddock's mercantile store and found his friend in what appeared to be, a deep conversation with Jesse Winthrop. "Howdy," he said. It was early afternoon and the temperature said late spring. "Spring is with us for another day or two. Must be important business to get you away from your anvil, Jesse."

"Heard some wild stories about you earlier, Jack Slater," Winthrop said. "Ricky Burdick just left."

"Well, he was there, Jesse, so you probably got

the story straight. Seems as though Amos Warren has a burr stuck deep in his blanket, made some ignorant comments to Rob and I let fly. It got nasty quick, but started long before the words were flung about. Started with Warren getting Belafleur's blood up."

"How far is this going to go, Jack?" Valley Paddock was responsible for Jack Slater being a Nevada rancher, had helped him buy his first holding after meeting him in Cheyenne, Wyoming Territory. "Burdick seems to think that Warren might want some kind of revenge after the beating you gave him."

"I'd bet on it," Slater said. "That's the kind of skunk he is." He took a moment to look into Valley Paddock's eyes. Was it concern he saw? Or was Paddock trying to tell him something? "Why don't we wander down the street and get Horseface Hawkins involved in these discussions."

It was a quick walk on a fine spring day. Even the wind had a touch of gentle to it. "Sure glad Wes Trimble's herd got back safely." Jack said. "Fool attempt to take that many head and move them almost through town. He was still angry at the meetings."

"He's fuming and positive that Warren was behind the heist. That one outlaw that I recognized, the one who came into my store," Paddock said, "was also recognized as a Warren hand. Recent hire, though. Can't understand what's going on."

"Sheriff says those four came in from Colorado. You're worried about something, old friend, and I don't think it has that much to do with Amos burning me out." Jack nodded to Horseface Hawkins to fill everyone's glasses. "We're a thirsty bunch, Horseface. Keep 'em coming and join us, please."

"I've been among those gleefully getting ready to welcome the new century coming our way in a couple of years, Jack." Valley Paddock shook his head slowly. "The new technology that's sweeping the country, the wonderful progress we're making toward civilizing our frontier." Valley stopped and shook his head again.

"You've always been an optimist, Mr. Paddock, sir," Jack laughed. "And now, you're seeing a cattle rustling gang come right through your town, a ranching neighbor of ours threatening to burn out another neighbor, and you think we're sliding back to the dangerous times of the early frontier."

"In a nutshell, Jack Slater. Couldn't have said it better. So what are you going to do about it?" Valley had a satisfied look on his face. He got Slater to outline the problem and made it Slater's responsibility to clean up the mess. A good politician is hard to beat.

Jesse Winthrop was laughing along with Horseface Hawkins. "It's your problem now, Jack," he said. The blacksmith downed his beer and looked for Horseface to pour some more. "Let's start with the rustling. Those boys that come through here were working from a plan is what I'm thinking. Cut the fences on pastured cattle and run them all night long through rough country, but to where? Where were they taking that fair size herd?"

"That's what everyone at the Elko meetings were talking about, Jesse," Jack said. "Ted Wilson seems to think this is a modern type of rustling. Most rustling is used by poor men looking to build their herds, or gangs looking for a quick sale of cattle with altered brands."

"That's exactly right, Slater." Horseface Hawkins limped down the bar and brought a stool back up to where he could sit, take the load off his busted up legs. "Won't work in today's new world, Paddock's world. No big market for rustled cattle today."

"That's exactly what Wilson was saying," Jack said. "He thinks this gang is moving cattle through a feedlot to a packing house and selling boxes of cut-up beef, refrigerated or frozen. Shipping it to markets by way of the railroad."

There was absolute silence in the bar as each man tried to put what Jack said into perspective. The silence was broken by the sound of horses being ridden up to the front of the Alabama House Saloon. "Company coming, boys. Let's talk about this a little later," Horseface said. "A most interesting idea, though. There's your modernity, Valley Paddock," he cackled.

Two dust covered buckaroos came through the heavy doors and walked to the end of the bar. "How about some of that fine whiskey of yours, Hosrseface?" It was Jake Winters, a long-time Amos Warren hand.

"Coming right up, Jake." Horseface took a quick look down the bar at Jack Slater and poured the two some bourbon. "Eight years old, Jake. About the best there is west of the Rocky Mountains."

"Oh, my," Will Austin said, easing a sip down his throat. "Sure ain't for swillin'."

"What brings a couple of Warren hands to town on a workin' day?" Jesse Winthrop said. He made sure he made the connection of them to Warren, just in case Slater wasn't aware of who they were.

"I got to get back," Jack said. He tried to be casual as he finished a beer, slapped Valley Paddock's shoulders, and nodded to Winthrop and Hawkins. "Work day, you said," he laughed.

"Wasn't that Slater?" Austin asked. They heard Slater's horse move off at a walk.

"In person," Jake Winters said.

"I gotta talk to him," Austin said. "I ain't ridin' for the Warren brand no more, Winters. Pick up whatever I got coming and leave it with Horseface here, if you don't mind." He finished what was left of the good whiskey and walked out. He didn't notice Jesse Winthrop and Valley Paddock both tense up some.

"Wonder where he's going?" Valley muttered. "Should we follow?" Winthrop shook him off.

Jake sat at the end of the bar, quiet and contemplative. *Life ain't gonna be nice for a long time to come.* He thought. *If I was to do the right thing, what would it be? Ride out with old Will? Ride back to tell Warren?* He chuckled softly. *Or just ride out.*

11

It took Will Austin just ten minutes to catch up to Jack Slater. "Mr. Slater." He called out, riding up alongside the big man. "Need to talk, sir."

"Don't mean to be rude, sir, but what would a Warren hand want to talk to me about? You bringing trouble?" He looked over at the man with the deep Texas drawl and saw fear, not anger or wrath. "I thrive on trouble, so make your move." Slater saw a man in his thirties, tall and lean, bronzed from years in the saddle. *This is strange. A Warren man, out of nowhere wants to talk? Talk? Anything more than talk and it's gonna get loud out here. Don't know what it is about these Texas drovers, but I can spot 'em a mile away. I'll bet this old boy would give Cactus Jack a run for his money on telling stories around the campfire.*

"Ain't bringing trouble, Mr. Slater, but I do want to talk about trouble. Not from me, though." He had a boyish smile on his face and Jack pulled his horse back to a walk. "I come in peace, sir. I just quit the Warren brand and I ain't looking for a job, neither. Name's Austin, Will Austin,"

"Glad to meet you, Austin. I'll take you at your word. Can we ride and talk?"

"We could, but I'd feel more comfortable talking over a cup of coffee. I'm mighty confused at the moment. Things I ain't never thought about are happening, and I need to know what's right and what ain't."

"Just about the hardest question there is, sometimes." Jack had to laugh. "Been there myself a time or two. The ranch is a couple miles in front of us and our housekeeper should have coffee cooking. Follow me, Mr. Austin. It's a good day to shake out these big critters we're riding." It was almost a race down that well used roadway, right up to the long driveway.

They turned in and rode the rest of the way in at a comfortable lope. Jack saw Andy Pettigrew standing at the front of the barn, rifle in hand and waved him off. "Can you take care of the horses, Andy? Mr. Austin and I have some talking to do. Jack and Rob out on the fences?"

"Yes, sir. The whole crew's out on the fences." Pettigrew had a strange look on his face as he walked the horses in. *Unless I'm just an old fool*

seein' a mirage, that old boy works for Amos War-
ren. I've seen just about everything a man can see,
but I ain't never see'd this.

Jack led Will Austin into the warm kitchen and introduced him to Wanda Camacho. "We could use some hot coffee, Wanda."

"I'll have some fresh biscuits coming out of the oven in a couple of minutes, too. Glad you're back safe." She gave the stranger called Will Austin long look, gave him a smile, too. "Where's the family?"

"Won't be too far behind me. I'm sure they're taking their time." He got seated and Wanda poured coffee for them. "So, let's start from the beginning, shall we, Mr. Austin? You sound like a Texan to me. You a drover?"

"A good one, Mr Slater. West Texas mostly. Made three drives north, saw some beautiful land, and worked for good brands. Can't say that today." He shook his head and took a long pull on the coffee mug. He nodded his thanks to Wanda, but he couldn't smile.

Slater saw a storm spread across the man's face. Austin took another drink of coffee and had a hard time looking Jack in the face. "This is the hardest thing I think I've ever had to say." He stood up and walked to the door, turned and sat back down. "I think Mr. Warren is looking to burn you out, Mr. Slater. At least, that's what he said this morning." He looked up, sadness dripping from his large brown eyes.

Slater tried his best not to show surprise, anger, or fear, but let his mind work on what was said. *I gave Amos Warren the beating of his life last night, Rob shot his foreman, and he lost another man, too. I could understand anger and maybe mouthing it off some to the crew, but looking into this man's eyes, Warren's anger might go back some, what he's saying might not just be bad talk.*

"I don't understand what's going on." Austin looked right at Slater. "Sonny Belafleur was shot and is in jail, neighbors' herds are being rustled, and Warren men are involved. I don't want anything to do with any of it."

"What are you going to do, Austin? You said you weren't looking for a job."

"Ain't. Maybe drift down to Arizona or New Mexico. Good country, south. I've always enjoyed seeing new country." He took another long drink of hot coffee, but was looking Jack in the eye. "I just felt it would be wrong ridin' off without you knowin' what might be comin' at you."

"You're a good man, Mr. Austin. It is good country down south," Jack said. He sat back in his chair, looking at this sun-baked, wind-creased buckaroo, and wondered just how much he knew about Warren's plans. Wondered, too if the man might be a plant, that in reality he is looking for a job. The kind of job where he could get information back to Warren. *Best way to get an answer is to just call him out, not sit here like a lump of coal.* Jack smiled at the thought.

"I'm in a bit of an awkward position, here, Austin. I'm most grateful for you bringing me this information."

"And you're worried that I might have been sent here to get a job and find out things for Mr. Warren. Right?" Will Austin said it with an ironic chuckle. "I understand, sir. I'm a bit confused myself. You see, me and Jake Winters, the man I was with in the saloon back there, were sent here to find out what we could about your place. No way I could do that. Jake ain't going to, either."

Austin looked around the large, open kitchen and smiled. "I don't mind a good fight but I've always thought there should be something come out of it. What Warren wants to do ain't a good fight, Mr. Slater. It's ugly, sinful." It looked like he was trying to get the scowl and anger off his face.

"I'm also confused about the rustling that's been going on. We had lots of rustling in Texas with people coming in, picking critters off the range to start their herds, even gangs of outlaws, but what were those men going to do with Mr. Trimble's beef? Surely couldn't sell them."

That question settled it for Slater. A good cow man is always aware that what he's raising is a cash crop. He wants his beef to be the tastiest, tenderest piece of meat in the land. A good side of beef without a market ain't no different than a wilted radish sitting in the hot sun. *This long tall Texan is a cow man.*

"I'm gonna go way out on a limb here, Mr. Austin. Don't ask me why, but I see a lively mind, a good cow man, and an honest one. Why don't you stay in this fine country and go to work for me. I've about got it in my craw that Warren's involved in these cattle thefts and uses his hatred of fences as an excuse.

"Somebody's making lots of money right now, on other people's beef and I want to be one of those that puts a stop to it. Have you met my foreman, Cactus Jack Faraday?"

"No, but I've sure heard plenty about him and your son, Rob. Tough hombres, Mr. Slater. Sonny Belafleur had a great hate for both of them. Is it true your son is the one who shot Belafleur?"

"No doubt about that. Lot a people saw it. Let's get our horses and ride out and find those yahoos. I haven't heard a no about my idea, either."

"Ain't said yes," Austin said. He had a nice smile plastered across his face. He was holding the door for Jack, and said, "Yet. We'll ride out and I'll do some serious thinkin'. Something that comes when you make those long and lonely trail drives across west Texas. Got a lot of time for thinkin'."

Slater liked the easy way Austin had with conversation, but still had a doubt or two running up and down his back bone. *It would be a fearsome group. Rob, Cactus Jack, and Will Austin.* "What have you heard, direct, from any of the Warren hands about the rustling going on? You said you thought Warren was involved. Why?"

"Got nothin' direct, Mr. Slater. It's just that Sonny Belafleur will draw out a hand or two to work with some men hired to move cattle, only to find out later they helped rustle cattle. Warren has to know or be involved too, wouldn't you think?"

"I do. You sure you're up to what we're leading ourselves into?" They were riding through good grass and deep sage brush, scattered stands of pine and scrub cedar, late in a spring day. "It got mean fast last night and that surely won't be the last time." He pulled his horse to a stop and pointed off to the north. "There's Cactus and Rob. Ride slightly in front of me so they don't get the wrong idea of why we're together." They both had to chuckle at that and Will Austin led Jack up to the pair.

"Home at last, Liz. I'm actually tired from this trip. That was so scary last night." Mims was getting Seth, little Jack, and Maybelle down from the wagon.

They had been fidgety for the last hour or more and needed time to romp and get tired. Little Jack, still a baby, needed food and changing, and was telling the world about it. "Glad when these youngsters are old enough to ride horses on trips like these."

"I was so scared when that man came after Rob," Liz said. "He and Papa Jack are quite a team, aren't they? Are we going to be in danger?"

"A team? Yes, and family. Life is full of danger, Liz," Mims said. "But the answer is, probably. That fat old Mr. Warren is a trouble maker and he won't take kindly to the beating Jack gave him or to Rob shooting his ranch foreman. We'll need to listen to what the men say. Jack's upset with all the thefts of beef going on and said he thought that Warren just might be mixed up in it."

"I've been watching how you take care of your kids, Mims. You're a wonderful mother."

"I've been a mama since I was ten-years-old, Liz. Old Mr. Jablonski wasn't married, didn't like children, and the only reason he adopted us was so we could work his farm. Ask Jack. I was the mama." She couldn't hold in the laugh and nudged Maybelle up the stairs to get the door open.

It took a couple of hours to put away everything from the trip, get the children down for a short nap before supper, and still have time for biscuits with butter and jam and a full pot of hot coffee. "What have you got for us tonight, Wanda? I could eat half a ton," Mims asked, "and I know Liz will eat even more."

"I put a lamb stew on, Mims. Used the biggest cast iron Dutch oven we have and it's full to over-flowing some. The mister brought a man to the house and I think we'll have a guest at the table, too. He talked like he was from Texas and you know how I feel about Texas."

"That man's in trouble, Liz." Mims was laughing. "Is he a long tall skinny buckaroo with shiny black hair and dark eyes, Wanda? Or short and fat with gray hair?"

"Humph," Wanda snorted and turned back to the stove. "Wavy brown hair and big brown eyes," she muttered ever so quietly and Mims and Liz both laughed right out. "Cain't hep it, Mims. I like them Texans."

12

"My mama used to make stew like that," Will Austin said. Those big brown Texas eyes were eating up Wanda Camacho and she couldn't keep her eyes off of him, either. "Great chunks of meat and lots of potatoes. Enough gravy to drown a dozen biscuits and soft butter to help it along." His eyes were sparkling and Wanda's smile was bright enough to be seen in Skelton, five miles away.

There was no doubt in anyone's mind what was going on between the two and Cactus Jack was having a terrible time holding in the guffaws. Rob reached over and poked him and that's all it took. Cactus, Rob, Jack, and Two-dog were roaring, Austin was beet red and Mims was trying to get things back into some semblance of order.

Wanda Camacho was sitting across the long table from Will Austin and ducked her head, hiding her wide and beautiful smile. "Thank you," she whispered. *Oh, my heavens, I think I'm back in Laredo.*

Cactus Jack led a second round of laughter and watched both Will Austin and Wanda try to hide their embarrassment. "Better get used to it, Texas," Cactus said. Faraday was also from Texas and the two partnered up quick on the ride back to the home ranch. It was time to change the subject.

"You ever ride for Goodnight or any of them big boys down there?"

"Made one season with somebody from Wichita Falls. 'Bout the biggest drive I made, I guess. Like to see new country," he chuckled. "With a table filled like this, I just may have found my home place, though." He looked right into Wanda's eyes and she took in a fast breath of air.

"Let's see if we can figure out this rustling problem over a glass of brandy, gentlemen." The supper-time fun was over, it was time to go back to work. Enough frivolity. "If you have apple pie, Wanda, we would like a slice each, in the living room, please." Slater led the men into the great room where they found leather arm chairs near the blazing fireplace. Rob brought glasses and a decanter of brandy.

"If you, Mr. Austin, were going to steal fifty head of my best beef, where would you take them and what would you do with them?"

"First off, I wouldn't," Will answered with a laugh. "But realistically? There simply ain't any market for stolen cattle, Mr. Slater."

"Around here, I'm called Jack, Will." Austin liked that and gave him a nod. "That's been my point from the start. Why steal someone's cattle if you can't sell 'em or eat 'em. Now, my good friend Ted Wilson has a theory that makes good sense. Not that many years ago, beef was sent to the big packing houses in Chicago and the east, but that isn't so, now."

"You're right, Jack," Austin said. He looked around at Cactus Jack and Rob. "Railroads still carry the beef, but they're in boxes, frozen or just refrigerated. That's what killed the big drives, too. Railroads expanded and there are packing houses close to good beef country now."

"This new century coming up on us is gonna be hard to live in, Jack," Cactus said. "So you're buying into that idea that the stolen cattle is slaughtered right here in the county and shipped out cut and frozen?"

"I am," Jack said. "The big feedlot in Elko has a packing house right next door and most of the beef we sell to the feedlot ends up there. Some is shipped out live, but not much. Our big market is Reno, Carson City, and Virginia City. There are feedlots and packing houses springing up wherever beef is raised."

"Art Simpson owns the Elko Feedlot, Dad. I don't think there's a more honest man in the county. I can't picture him buying stolen beef. Just can't," Rob said. "Old Shorty Watson at the Elko slaughter house would never take a mis-branded calf. I think Ted Wilson's idea might hold water if it wasn't for Simpson and Watson."

"I tend to go along with Rob on this, Jack," Cactus said. "Those two men are honest as the day. Railroad won't ship cattle without proper paperwork and branding, either. I'm not sure that's where these outlaws are getting rid of their stolen stock. Indians ain't getting' any either. They got some fine herds of their own, now."

"These outlaws obviously have a market," Slater said. He was frustrated and sat back in his chair, staring into the fire. "Rob, you almost got sucked into stealing cattle. Where were they taking those beeves?"

"I remember that," Rob said. "They only took three or four animals and had them pre-sold to down and out families. Not the same."

"There's a Warren man who seems to work more for Sonny Belafleur than Warren," Will Austin said. "He calls himself Stormy, don't know what his real name is. He's always around the place but isn't a working hand. He rides off from time to time with others who aren't really Warren hands. Also Odie Jackson and the Forbes brothers, though Toby Forbes was killed when Belafleur got shot."

"You might be on to something, Will. Keep going."

"Toby Forbes was killed the other night, but his brother Skinny was almost Belafleur's right hand man and Three-toes Jacobs and Odie Jackson are the others. They often just ride off and won't be seen for a few days or even more. Don't know where they go."

"I can just about tell you," Cactus said. "If you matched when they rode off to when cattle went missing, you'd know."

"Are those men at the Warren place now?" Jack asked.

"Nope. Didn't come back with us from Elko. Stormy's there because he didn't go to Elko, but none of the others." Will Austin was getting the picture and didn't like what he saw. "It appears that I may have taken part in some cattle rustling, Jack. How do we put a stop to it?"

"Where did you take the cattle, Will?"

"Didn't. Herded 'em out of a pasture and then the Warren men were thanked and sent home. Don't know where they drove 'em off to."

"Let's all sleep on this," Jack said. "Been one long day for all of us. Cactus, in the morning put Pettigrew on the fences with the crew and the four of us need to take a ride into Skelton. I've got an idea."

Blake Wilson was pacing circles around his desk in the feedlot office, waiting for word to come from Odie Jackson. Jackson was the man he picked to kill Sonny Belafleur and it had been three days now. *It's getting so you can't count on anyone. Belafleur, always so sure of himself, shot by a boy. Jackson, happy to take Sonny's place, but where is he? Three days on a job that shouldn't take two hours.*

The late spring morning in Elko bloomed hot and humid, thunderheads already building as an opening scene for the coming summer months. Odie Jackson was in the Golden Oaks Saloon talking with Deputy Clyde Parks.

"I bet he ain't swaggering much in there," Jackson said.

Parks nodded with a knowing smile. "Not even a little bit. Worrying his hurt leg all the time, growling about killing him a Slater boy when he gets out. He ain't gettin' out from what I hear."

Odie cocked his head and asked why the lawman thought that. "Got a price on his head from what I heard. Sheriff's got enough security on that boy, but I imagine with the right price he could get hisself killed."

Jackson's idea of pretending to be drunk and getting thrown in jail went out the window and he decided to wait until they were taking him to court. Easier to kill him as he was moved from the jail to court. "What did they charge him with?"

"Some kind of assault. He had his gun out and was firing it when he was shot. Can't claim self-defense," the deputy laughed. "Justice of the peace will probably just leave him in the county lockup for a couple of months."

"Like to sit in on that trial," Odie Jackson said.

"Well, if you're still in town, it'll happen tomorrow morning. Little lady's waiting for me. Gotta go," he said. Odie watched him walk out the door, letting his mind start to work on tomorrow.

"Tomorrow morning, eh?" He was muttering, putting a plan together. He finished his beer and headed for his little camp a mile or so out of town. "How did the word get out that someone might be gunning for old Sonny? Blake Wilson or Skinny Forbes?" Odie Jackson was muttering up a storm as he put together a plan to kill Sonny Belafleur before he got to court.

13

Court usually convened at ten each morning and the prisoners, chained to each other at the waist, were paraded the long block from the jail to the courthouse. There would be a few drunks left over from the night before to cheer them on, some street urchins to throw dirt at them, and often a preacher scolding them for their sins.

The good women of the town would be able to sneer at the hapless men and women, letting all of Elko know that neither they nor their men would ever be in such a lineup. There was always just a touch of gaiety to the procession as well.

Sheriff Mossy Peabody took great pleasure leading the parade and had two or three deputies urging the prisoners on. Peabody was a showboat of a sheriff, rode a horse that did more prancing than running, dressed as if for court, not catching outlaws, and was up for re-election in just a year.

The prisoners were chained together at the waist and the more dangerous had their feet in shackles. Because of attitude problems, probably, the wounded Sonny Belafleur was among the shackled despite his leg wound. He was last in line. He was cussing loud and long, stumbling as best he could with his leg wrapped in bloody bandages, and would kill anyone who came close.

He had several day's growth of whiskers, was still wearing the same clothes he had on for the cattlemen's festivities, and looked haggard. His head was wrapped in bloody bandages that were more than filthy, from his encounters with Rob Slater.

Odie Jackson stood at the window, inside the Golden Eagle Saloon, a sly grin on his face as he watched the parade make its way onward. The drunk trick wouldn't have worked to get his man before, but this was different. He had it timed, he thought and stumbled out of the saloon, knocking over a woman holding some packages, and careened off another man, giving him a solid bump.

"Ooh!" The woman cried out, spilling her packages and falling to a knee.

"Be careful, you oaf!" The gentleman snarled, pushing Odie hard. Jackson seemed to almost fall off the board sidewalk, out into the street and took a tumble just as Sonny Belafleur came by. Belafleur went down in a heap, taking three of the prisoners in front of him to the ground as well. A knife flashed in the morning sun and found its home in Sonny's heart.

Odie Jackson got to his feet fast, grabbed a deputy for balance, bounced off a man rushing to help, and made his way through the crowd and down a dark alley next to the saloon. It was all over in just seconds, but almost a full minute before anyone realized that Sonny Belafleur was never getting up.

Mossy Peabody was given half a dozen different descriptions of the drunk who caused the chaos, but no one was able to give a name. Within half an hour Odie Jackson had his little camp packed up and was riding for the feedlot near Halleck, a wide smile across his outlaw face. *Maybe we can bring some order back into our little operation now that Mr. Ego isn't making all the plans.*

Jack Slater took the lead as he, Cactus Jack, Rob, and Will Austin rode into Skelton in the late morning. They pulled their horses up in front of Jesse Winthrop's blacksmith barn. "Morning, Jesse. Seen Rick Burdick around this morning?"

"He's down at Paddock's, palavering about something. Leave the horses, I'll take care of them. That way we can have a cold one when Horseface gets open."

Jack and the crew were still laughing as they walked into Valley Paddock's large emporium. "Jack Slater." Valley hollered out. "Just the man we were talking about." Valley had a large table in the back of his store, near the pot-belly stove and he and Deputy Sheriff Rick Burdick were sitting with coffee cups in front of them. "Sit down."

"Sonny Belafleur is dead, Jack." Burdick looked across at Jack, then Rob.

"From a leg wound?" Rob sat very quiet, thinking he had killed the man. "I didn't think it was that serious."

"According to the wire I got half an hour ago, he was stabbed to death while they were taking him to court this morning." Burdick looked around the table and realized Will Austin, a Warren man was with Slater's crew. "What's this?"

"Might as well spread it about, I guess," Jack said. "Meet my new man, Rick. Amos Warren ain't gonna like this. Tell me about what happened to Belafleur. Sounds like someone didn't want that outlaw around anymore."

"A man, supposedly drunk, came stumbling out of the crowd, knocking people about, fell into Sonny and stabbed him. Got away before anyone even knew Sonny was dead." Burdick was shaking his head and looked over to Austin, almost smiling. "Give you any ideas, Will?"

"Matter of fact, it does." He said. "One of the men who is always around but isn't a Warren hand is Odie Jackson, always playing with his knife. Whipping it about. He's a real fool with that thing and has been known to threaten more than one man with it. Five-ten, One fifty, dark blond hair and no mustachio."

"That was one of the descriptions," Burdick said. He still had a quizzical look, wondering what brought Austin to the Slater camp.

"The reason we're in town, Rick, is to pick your brain on a couple of things. Sorry to hear about Sonny Belafleur, but his loss isn't that great in my world," Jack said. "Other than the Elko feedlot and packing house, are there any others in the county?"

"Sure, Jack. There's a small feedlot at Halleck and a new packing house built right next door. Blake Wilson has the feedlot and is managing the packing house for the owner, who I think, lives in San Francisco. Why?"

"Just working on an idea that Ted Wilson has about the rustling going on." Jack looked around at everyone, his eyes asking if anyone had any information on this Halleck operation. "Halleck is a watering stop for the trains and the road south out of there leads into the Ruby Valley. Good place for a feedlot."

"It isn't as big as Simpson's in Elko, but I'm sure the boys north and south of there, ship out of Halleck." Rick Burdick was more than interested in what Jack was talking about. "Been some small time beef stealing in the Ruby Valley, too." He looked up at the ceiling, "Star Valley's been hit with some losses, too."

"Your idea of small time is what?" Jack asked.

"Oh, fifteen, twenty head. Not whole herds like those fools who rustled Trimbles' place." Burdick got up and stretched. "Gotta make some rounds, gentlemen. Don't worry, Rob, you didn't kill Belafleur and Austin? You are gonna be a bunch happier riding with Slater." The deputy walked out, grabbing the last of the sweet rolls on the table.

"Was there any talk about Halleck around the bunk house at Warren's?" Jack asked Will Austin. "I think we need to know a little bit more about that operation."

"No, not about Halleck, but I've heard Sonny Belafleur use the name Blake Wilson. Can't remember just what he might have been talking about, though."

"The big houses in Chicago have been using the refrigerated rail cars for some time. They move tons of boxed beef. It isn't really that new," Rob Slater said. "It never would have entered my mind though, about using that idea to move stolen beef."

"I think it might be understood by our outlaw friends, Rob," Jack said. "Let's help Horseface

Hawkins get open and have a cold beer. We have to get back to the ranch and pack up for a little ride to Halleck, I think. Cactus, you bring Austin up to speed on our operation while Rob and I are gone."

It was a long ride back to the Warren spread and Jake Winters had more than one fight with himself on the way. The first fight was to even ride back after Will Austin just walked off and left him. *Austin was right. I ain't gonna burn out a neighbor, either. So why am I riding back?* Part of it was the pay and getting two hot meals a day. Part of it was, he was getting a little long in the tooth and worried about getting another job.

Worn out old buckaroos could look forward to being swampers for a place to flop down, or worse. Most had no other skills. They could ride anything with four feet, but of course they left the brand because of age. They could rope, but, what is it they would rope. Smart ones ended up being the hired hand with clever stories around the camp fire.

Is it wrong for a man to think of his own welfare over what might be considered a more ethical approach? In Winters' case, getting paid and fed well but being expected to commit a serious crime against a neighbor? One might call it a fight between pragmatism and philosophy.

The worst part of the answer was, he was afraid of Amos Warren's temper. Afraid of who might be named foreman to replace Sonny Belafleur. Belafleur was sadistic, similar to Warren, and Warren was sure to replace him with someone equally mean and vicious. "Warren's sure as all get-out going to take his anger out on me when I tell him about Austin," Winters muttered.

Most of the Warren crew were gathered near the large corral, listening to another of Amos Warren's harangues as Jake Winters rode in. "Well, you're back early. Find out anything about the Slater place? Where's Austin?" The color was rising on Amos Warren's bulging neck and Jake Winters wanted to turn his horse and ride out fast. Instead he stepped down from the saddle.

"Got some bad news, Mr. Warren. Will Austin quit and rode off when we got to Skelton."

Along with Warren were five men along the corral fence and there wasn't a sound for several moments. Amos took two fast steps toward Jake who turned and tried to get his horse between them. "Don't be taking your anger out on me, Mr. Warren," he almost whimpered. "It weren't me that rode off."

"No, of course it wasn't," Warren said. "Tell me what happened and don't be lyin'." He glared at Winters. "Well? Tell me now, Winters." He took another step closer and Jake Winters started talking fast. He told about what they heard in the Alabama House Saloon, how Jack Slater rode off and Austin followed.

"He rode out with Slater?" Amos Warren's anger exploded in loud and vile words. He showered Winters in the worst language a man could use, called him a coward for not following and killing the both of them, fired him and demanded he be off the property now.

"If I ever see you again, Winters, I'll kill you. I won't have a coward riding for the Warren brand. Get off my property now."

For the first time in many years, Jake Winters found his backbone. "I have pay coming, Mr. Warren."

"I'll show you what pay you have coming you miserable excuse for a man." He raised the quirt he always carried and slashed it across Winters' face, opening a long bloody gash. He slashed once, twice more, seeing Winters fall to the ground. But, it wasn't over. Jake Winters grabbed for his sidearm, pulled it and he and Amos Warren fired at the same time.

Jake Winters writhed in pain for just seconds before dying and Amos Warren was thrown back several feet with a bullet lodged deep in his left shoulder. He was trying to get on his feet when Three-toes Jacobs and another hand helped him up. "Let's get you in the house, Mr. Warren and get that looked at."

Three-toes nodded to the others to get Jake Winters' buried and get back to work. It would never be the same on the Warren property after, Jacobs knew. He also knew he had to get the word to Blake Wilson at the feedlot.

"Better ride for the doc," he yelled at Louie Bloom. It took three men to get Warren in the house and onto his bed. Warren was bleeding hard and Three-toes ripped his coat off and tore his shirt back to expose the wound.

Three-toes had worked on many more than just this one bullet wound and had the bleeding under control quickly. "The doc can take care of the rest of it," he murmured. "He's unconscious, boys, so we'll just let him sleep. The doc's gonna have a lot of trouble working through all that fat to find that tiny little slug."

The four men left the room chuckling on the one hand and wondering just what was going on, on the other. The boss shot and killed one of his hands after giving him a terrible thrashing and was wounded in turn. Another hand, sent to spy on a neighbor quit his job and maybe rode off with the neighbor. And, they don't have a foreman. More than one was planning on riding off later that day.

"Why aren't we on the main road north, Dad?" Rob asked. They were in the rocky foothills on the western flanks of the Ruby Mountains, nearing the entrance to the vast Lamoille Canyon that stretches deep into the Rubies. "Not making the best time threading our way like this."

"We're following the track the rustlers were using, Rob. Thought there might be something to give us a clue. It's a long drive, moving stolen cattle from the Skelton area to Halleck. They had to be planning to lay over somewhere, probably two or three times and yet not be seen."

"Doesn't make any sense to me, driving that many stolen cattle that far. I've been worrying on this ever since Ted Wilson brought up the idea of moving slaughtered beef. It must be very lucrative. There must be a lot of money involved, far more than just cattle on the hoof. It would also take someone with a deep knowledge of the beef market to arrange it all." Rob was a thinker, was trying to work out the details of finding a market for the packaged beef and the logistics of getting it moved safely.

"When they discovered refrigeration and freezing it really opened up the beef market. From a hide market to a meat market just because the meat can be kept cold. Amazing," Rob said. "Fresh beef can be bought in just every town and city because of it. Refrigeration created the idea of regional distributors, Dad. That must be how this works. Contracts with distributors."

"You're the amazing one, Rob," Jack said. He was looking the youngster right in the eye. "Your mother would be so proud of you. I'm mighty glad you're my son, but I wish your mother was still alive to see what a fine man you've grown into."

As they rode in silence across the broad mouth of the canyon, Jack spotted what looked like corrals where there shouldn't be any. "No ranches right around here. Let's look," he said. All they found were remnants of a previously used set of holding corrals. "Haven't seen any use for some time, but would hold a hundred or more head."

They continued their ride north to the Western Pacific rails. "Well, that was wasted time," Slater said, when they reached the well-used road running east and west. The road started in Missouri and ended in Sacramento.

"The chances of a stolen herd of cattle being seen would be great, I think," Rob said. He couldn't hold in the snicker. "This country isn't like the wide open spread of country in Texas and New Mexico. This has been populated for many years. It's open to a degree, but not to move large herds of stolen cattle."

They were still many miles out of Halleck when they ran out of daylight and made a nice camp in a stand of cottonwood trees. "We'll be in Halleck tomorrow, Dad. We can't just ride up to the packing house and ask about stolen beef." Rob Slater was chuckling, thinking about that.

"I think we'll start in the village, Rob. Never know what you can learn from the local man standing behind the bar at a busy saloon."

14

They followed the Halleck railroad siding toward a set of warehouses on the outskirts of the little town. There were ranch supply, farm implement, lumber and heavy equipment warehouses and yards, and found a second siding running right up to the feedlot. There was a rail side loading dock at the packing house, too. Jack and Rob rode on past and into the heart of the little village. Like most small towns and villages, it was made up of a feed and implement store, stables and blacksmith, dry goods and mercantile shops, and a hotel-saloon. "There's the busy saloon you were talking about," Rob joshed.

"We'll get a room and check things out," Jack said. "Chances are good that I'll know someone, so there's no need to try to be secret about our visit. It would be nice to meet someone who works at either the feedlot or the packing house."

It was late on what was a hot spring day when Jack and Rob stood at the bar in the Halleck Hotel Saloon and Music Palace. "How about a couple of cold ones to wash the dust down," Jack said to the barman. He was a rotund fellow, red in the fat cheeks and bright in the pudgy little brown eyes, and he wore a grand walrus mustache that spread even further when prodded by a generous smile.

"Comin' right atcha, boys." He filled two large schooners and slid them down the long oak bar with precision. "Want a bottle to go with 'em?"

"No, we'll save that for a little later. This place yours, is it?"

"No, Terry Johnson owns this and most of the other businesses here in town. Name's Bill Anderson, but my friends call me Hooter."

"Nice to meet you, Hooter. Hoping to maybe run into a feller named Wilson. Blake Wilson. He come this way?" Jack was giving the saloon a good look and found it clean and functional, not gaudy or phony.

Gambling took place in the front of the saloon while food was served in the back. There was a small stage and off to the side of it, a piano with two empty stools, the second one probably for a banjo player. Oil lamps hung in wagon wheels suspended from a high ceiling and there was a doorway that led into the hotel lobby.

"Wilson don't come in here that often. I don't think we're quite good enough for that gentleman's tastes. Hope you're not a close friend," the barman said. He had an impish smile spreading across a generous face.

Jack had to chuckle. "No, just interested in his business. Looked like a busy feedlot when we rode by."

"A couple of his hands will probably come in a little later. They ain't too friendly, but you might learn something. You'll want to stay away from a feller named Odie Jackson. Got a mean temper loves to flash that knife of his."

"That's the second time we've heard that name, Rob." He and Rob watched the heavy doors swing open and three men come in. "Might be the crew now"

"It is indeed," the barman said. "Tall skinny one is named Duke something. Not sure I ever heard a last name. Probably the easiest of the bunch to get along with." The large gentleman walked down the bar to welcome the new customers.

"Let's see what we can pick up from conversation first and then decide if we want to talk to anyone," Jack said.

He needn't have, as the tall Duke gentleman walked right up to Slater. "Old Hooter there said you wanted to talk about the feedlot. Name's Duke Winston. Lookin' to bring some beef in, are you?"

"Might just be, Duke. Name's Slater, Jack Slater, and this is my son, Rob. Looked like a busy place as we rode in earlier."

"Much more steady now that the packing house is operating. Feedlots are mostly seasonal, but with that facility, we can take cattle, sheep, and hogs all year long. I've heard your name, I think," Duke said. "Your place is on the west side of the Rubies, ain't it?"

"That's the place, but we're looking at some property in the Ruby Valley," Jack lied. "Your feedlot would be nice and close." Jack motioned for more drinks and was surprised at how open Duke Winston was. He anticipated someone unwilling to disclose anything at all about the operations.

"The packing house is fully operational now?" Jack asked.

"Makin' ice and freezin' beef," Duke laughed. "Sure a big change from just a few years ago."

He was interrupted by another man who barged his way into the conversation. "You're askin' a lot of questions, mister. You'd be better off talkin' to Mr. Wilson instead of one of the hired hands. Go drink with the boys, Duke."

Duke glared at the demand, stood silent for a moment or two, like he was thinking hard about arguing with the man, but walked on back down the bar. "Didn't catch your name," Slater said. "You're not just a hired hand yourself?" The prod caught Odie Jackson by surprise. Most men didn't talk back to him like that. After all, he was one of Wilson's special men.

"Name's Jackson and I'm an associate of Blake Wilson's. Mr. Wilson don't much care for people pokin' their noses into his business."

"Well, Mr. Jackson, I don't much care for people tellin' me who I can talk to or who I can't. Maybe you should mind your own business and let me mind mine." Slater didn't raise his voice or appear angry and Rob knew that was a sign that anything could explode at any moment. "I'm looking to maybe move some cattle and needed some answers. You got yourself a bad attitude, sir."

"And you got yourself a bag full of trouble, mister. Ain't nobody talks to me that way." Odie Jackson reached for the heavy Bowie knife at his belt and felt the barrel of a big Colt pressed to the back of his neck.

"Just flinch, mister. Please. I ain't shot nobody in some time." Rob was grinning at Jack, but his voice wasn't. Jack reached out and took the knife from its scabbard and laid it on top of the bar. "You want to continue this conversation with my dad, you be a gentleman."

The feedlot men were tensed and ready for something to happen. They had seen Odie Jackson too many times destroy an evening's enjoyment at

the bar. Would they back him this time or maybe
it would be better to let that young feller just go
ahead and shoot him?

Duke Winston stepped forward. "Easy, Mr.
Slater. No need for this to go any further." He
stood a good five inches taller than Jackson, had
him by twenty pounds or more, and watched Rob
Slater ease the hammer back down.

"Jackson, you might swing some weight at the
feedlot, but not after hours in the saloon. Me and the
boys here, just want some quiet times and cold beer."

"Blake Wilson's gonna hear about this," Odie Jackson snarled, but didn't move, feeling that cold iron still
pressing on his neck. Rob eased the gun down and
back, into its leather, but kept his grip on it.

"You tell your Blake Wilson that Jack Slater will
pay a call on him tomorrow morning. Rob, keep
that Colt in its pocket. Don't ever pull a knife on
me, Mr. Jackson. My son let you off easy."

Jackson reached for the knife and Hooter slid
it off the bar and onto a shelf down below. "You
can pick this up later, Jackson. Might be best if
you leave. Don't like cleaning up blood this early
of an evening." He turned to Slater.

"Afraid you've made yourself an enemy, Mr.
Slater." Hooter wasn't smiling as Odie Jackson
stormed from the barroom. "I'm not sure I'd make
that visit tomorrow morning, either."

Jack and Rob looked at each other and didn't have to say a word. They understood that they almost had to make that meeting, now.

"We might have some problems coming our way, Mr. Wilson," Odie Jackson said. They were in Wilson's office early in the morning. Jackson was angry, glaring at the former cattle agent. "Slater's in town."

"The way I understood, when Belafleur talked about him, he was Amos Warren's problem, not ours. What makes you think this Jack Slater would be our problem?" Blake Wilson was in a large leather covered chair by the fire despite it being a warm spring morning.

"It was Slater's kid that shot Belafleur. It was Slater's kid's wife that Belafleur and Toby Forbes were gonna have some fun with. Slater got tight with Duke Winston last night before I stepped in and called Winston off."

"Word I got," Wilson snickered, "was that Slater called you off. Sloppy work, Odie. Sloppy. All you did was catch Slater's attention, make him wonder why you would do what you did. That isn't the kind of thinking I want around here. I want you and Skinny Forbes out of here today. Your only job is to find me cattle not run protection. I'm quite capable of protecting myself."

He turned away from Jackson, ignored him until the angry outlaw stormed out of the office. Wilson reached across his desk and rang a silver bell, bringing Ling Ho in at a run. "Find Duke Winters and bring him to me, Mr. Ling."

"You better calm yourself down, Odie. You running around with an anger like this is gonna get us both killed." Skinny Forbes was saddling his horse, watching Jackson kick everything in sight and cuss what he couldn't kick. "Why'd you go after Slater, anyway? He's Warren's problem, not ours."

"Don't you be talkin' down to me now, Skinny. Ain't no call for that." First Slater's kid puts a gun to his head, then Slater shames him in front of the Wilson crew and now, Skinny Forbes is doing the same thing. Odie Jackson had only one thought in his thin brain. Kill something, anything, soon.

"Get saddled, Odie. I want to check on some of those ranches in the South Fork Valley, see if we can pick up ten or so head. Also north of Deeth. That would get you back on the right side of Blake Wilson."

"I might just ride back to Warren's place and help him burn out Jack Slater. Ain't no man ever done that to me. That kid had a gun to the back of my head and Slater reached out and took my knife, Skinny. Took it right out of its leather and laid it on the bar and I couldn't do nothing but stand there and watch. I'm gonna kill me a couple of Slater men." Jackson was saddling his horse all the time he was talking.

"You can do that after we find some beef for Wilson. Let's move. Wilson was right, Odie and you know it. Wilson ain't got a problem with Slater. Warren has. Now, you've created a problem. You're lucky Wilson didn't fire you or shoot you."

"Why you," Jackson screamed, throwing himself at Skinny Forbes. They rolled around in the dirt and droppings and Skinny came out on top and slammed his fist into Jackson's face. He hit him at least four times before Jackson ran out of steam and couldn't fight back.

Forbes jumped to his feet and kicked Odie Jackson in the ribs, hard. "Get on that horse and ride off this property, Jackson. The next time I lay eyes on you, I'll kill you." He kicked him in the head. "Get up you coward and ride off now."

Odie Jackson fought to get on his feet and slowly climbed into the saddle. "Don't you be coming back this way, Jackson. You get smart with me or Blake Wilson and that Elko County Sheriff might learn a few things about you. Ride off, now, Jackson, while you can."

Skinny Forbes walked slowly to Blake Wilson's office with the bad news. Wilson paced around the office a couple of times, trying to cool his anger.

"Well, Mr. Forbes, at the moment it looks like it's just you and me on this project of mine. Get with Ricky Delgado and Three-toes, and see what can be saved. I have contracts that need to be filled. I had to let Duke Winston go this morning, also. Seems like we get 'em killed or run 'em off, eh?"

Forbes started to turn to leave and Wilson interrupted him. "Why is Amos Warren so angry with Jack Slater? What's the problem there? That feud, if that's what it is, is costing me money."

"In a nutshell, Mr. Wilson, Slater is far and away the better cattleman and Warren is just plain old jealous." Wilson shook his head and continued pacing. "He's jealous of everyone who has anything that he doesn't. Stupid man, Blake and Belafleur was more so getting is all tangled up the way we are." Forbes paced around for a time and stood by the fire.

"I've got a lead on a small herd of about twenty head in the Deeth area that I can bring in fast, Mr. Wilson."

"All right, get them first. It's the money that's most important, you realize," he laughed. They were both laughing when Forbes walked out. "I'm gonna have some angry distributors out there if I can't fill those contracts. I need cattle and more people, Skinny."

15

Jack and Rob were in the hotel stables saddling their horses when Duke Winters rode in. "Probably best not to visit with Blake Wilson this morning, Mr. Slater." He stepped down from his horse and tied it off. "Wilson sent Odie Jackson off and fired me for having a chat with you."

"That's interesting," Jack said. "You rode in to tell me this?" Jack was surprised by the encounter. He wondered if Blake Wilson was afraid that Slater might discover something, but also wondered if this Duke Winters might have some information, too.

"No, I didn't. I came in to send out some telegrams. The office is next door and I spotted you and your son."

"What are your plans, now, Winters?"

"After I let my family know I won't be here, I guess I'll ride into Elko and check with Shorty Watson or Art Simpson and the feedlot there.

They're usually short-handed. I don't think I would have lasted much longer here, anyway," Winters said. "There's something wrong about this operation but I don't know what it is."

"Rob, I think it's best we ride on home. We'll ride into Elko with you, Winters, if you don't mind our company?"

"I'd like that," Duke said. Jack smiled hoping that he would learn all about Blake Wilson's business on the way. It would take the better part of the day for the journey and plenty of time for talk.

"You said Wilson has some operations you don't understand? What would that be?" Jack came right to the point.

"Well, for one thing, they're a little lax on the brand inspections. I've worked more than one feedlot and brands are important. Wilson's more interested in bills of sale. He doesn't buy that many beeves from the ranchers, he buys them from a group of cattle buyers. Some of the brands are ugly, Mr. Slater, but the bills of sale seem legitimate."

"You ever done any cow work outside the feedlot?" Rob asked as they rode slowly out of town. "I love working cattle. Just about the time you think you know something about a cow, the cow does something it's never done before."

"They do that in the feedlots, too." Duke Winters had to laugh. It was the first time that morning.

"I grew up in Kansas working the railroad pens. It got mighty busy when those Texas herds came in. Those were wild cattle driven by wild drovers. Never worked a ranch, never branded a cow, but I can rope anything from either end," he laughed.

"If things don't work out for you at the Elko feedlot, come see me," Jack said. "We can always use another good man." Jack found himself liking this young man and particularly liking what he knew about Wilson's operation. "That's interesting about the bills of sale. I sell my cattle direct to the feedlot in Elko, never used a buyer, but I know they do exist. I would think, though, that the bill of sale should match the brand."

"Wilson is only interested in the bill of sale if it even slightly matches the brand. I'm not saying anything's illegal, Mr. Slater. I'm just not sure, though." He had a boyish grin on his face, shaking his head some, and shrugged. It was Rob who had to laugh.

"Tell me how this feedlot to packing house arrangement of Wilson's works," Rob asked. "Big change from shipping out live cattle. I'm fairly up on refrigeration and freezing, but have never been in one of the new packing houses."

Jack Slater enjoyed the rest of the ride into Elko listening to Rob and Duke talk about modern meat packing operations and sales. *Rob's gonna learn more about Wilson's operation than I ever could. I don't know what questions to even ask. I'm not looking forward to this next century bearing down on us.*

"You're gonna be fine, Amos." Doc Whitney had the bullet out and the skin all sewed back together. "I don't believe a word of your story, but it's your story, not mine, so you can keep it. Tell Three-toes to change the dressing and if it gets infected to wash it out with whiskey a couple of times. You ain't gonna die."

"You got a lot of good feelings in your heart, Doc," Warren said. "It don't mean nothin' to me whether you believe my story, but you'd better not be spreadin' wild lies about me when you get back to Skelton. I ain't gonna die and I hope I don't have to see your ugly face for a long time, either."

"I'll leave the bill with Three-toes." Whitney was still chuckling when he climbed into his little buggy for the ride back to Skelton. *He's a hard-nosed old buzzard that wouldn't know the truth if it hit him square in his fat face. Be interesting to know how he got shot like that. Sure wasn't from ropin' a steer and falling down.*

Three-toes Jacobs brought a bottle of brandy and a pot of coffee into Warren's bedroom. "Saw the doc ride off. You gonna live?"

"Long enough to bury you, Three-toes. And more than long enough to see Jack Slater chased out of this valley. Been some changes around here this past few days. Bring me up to date on people."

"Skinny Forbes and Odie Jackson never were on your payroll, Mr. Warren and they aren't around now that Sonny Belafleur is dead." Three-toes neglected to mention that he wasn't on Warren's regular payroll, either. "What we got right now is Ricky Delgado and Louie Bloom, but I'm not too sure of them, either. Belafleur played fast with your money, sometimes."

"How about Stormy?"

"He's with us, still." Stormy was an old cripple who spent time with the hogs and cleaning up. Not a cow hand.

"You, Ricky, Louie, and Stormy? From a full crew last week to this? Won't be no hands available in Skelton. I want you to ride into Elko and bring back at least four new men, six if you can find them."

"It's spring, Amos. Every decent hand in the country is workin'. Ain't gonna be no good ones walking around with empty pockets."

"Find what you can and don't be long about it. Git," Warren snarled.

Three-toes headed for the bunkhouse to pack up. "I gotta find Skinny Forbes or Odie Jackson and let them know what's happened." He took his time putting together a pack to fit behind the saddle for the easy ride to Elko. "I might just ride off and never look back."

Warren heaved his heavy body up on the side of the bed and reached for the brandy bottle, ignoring the coffee cup. It took until the third attempt for him to get to his feet and found the room doing a dance of its own. He stood as motionless as he could for a full minute before slowly making his way out of the bedroom and into the kitchen. Loss of blood combined with several snorts of hot brandy does that to a man.

I ain't got the cattle I should have because of that Jack Slater buying up good range land. Now, I ain't got the crew I should have because of Jack Slater's kid killing my foreman. He was counting the death toll. *Sonny's gone, Toby Forbes and Jake Winters are dead, and Willard Austin is now working for Slater. He won't have that job much longer. I have no idea where Skinny Forbes or Odie Jackson might be, either.*

He howled at his ranch cook to fix him a dinner and slowly made his way to a rocking chair on the kitchen porch, where he could look out at the corrals and barn. "All of my problems with this fine ranch of mine can be traced right back to Jack Slater. I gotta kill him and make it look like self-defense or an accident." He was muttering, almost speaking right out. "Gotta do it myself. Can't let one of these fools around here botch it up."

Sitting in his rocker was how Amos Warren ran his ranch just about every day of the week. He directed his men without having to actually move about, ride a horse, or swing a rope. He ate his mid-day dinner there and always had snacks of some kind handy.

Cookie brought out a platter of pork chops smothered in a deep brown gravy, along with half a dozen biscuits. "Got some early blackberries in a pie, boss, when you're through with this."

"Good, Cookie, good," Warren said. "Find that bottle of brandy for me, too."

"It's gonna be good to be home, Rob. Don't let me leave until fall roundup. I want a platter of beef steak from Wanda Camacho and a two-hour back rub from Mims." Jack and Rob left Duke Winston, at the Elko feedlot, spent the night at the Cattlemen's Hotel, and were off on the road to Skelton and home. "It was interesting, though, to learn how the packing houses have changed. You knew all about that, didn't you?"

"Been talking about it, but you and Cactus Jack don't always listen too close when I get to talking about modern ranching. Remember how I argued when I made you see your first piece of refrigeration equipment?" He was laughing, enjoying teasing his dad. He didn't get away with it very often. "It won't be that long and they'll have it down to where a person could have refrigeration right in their own homes."

"Bah," is all Jack could come up with. "You're right, though, Rob. About Wilson I mean. I think I understand how Blake Wilson is able to move stolen cattle all the way through the process without being caught. It's all in the paperwork I think."

Paperwork. How I hate that word but it's what keeps us on the right side of life, I guess. I can prove ownership because of it and I have to pay taxes because of it. And, now, we have a man who can steal cattle because of it.

"Paperwork such as bills of sale, brand inspections, and more than one signature?" Rob asked with a sly snicker. He was putting the cattle buyer in the equation. "Gotta have tight control if you're gonna get away with that. That cattle buyer has to be in on the process, for instance, rustling the cattle instead of buying them."

"The entire operation has to be led by Wilson," Jack said. "Sonny Belafleur must have been his key man. The buyer. I wonder where and how Amos Warren plays into all this?" Jack Slater was shaking his head trying to picture Warren having enough brains to fit in with what he knew about Blake Wilson. "I'm wondering if Warren is even aware that his crew is involved?"

"Sonny Belafleur and Toby Forbes ran Warren's ranch, Dad, not Amos Warren. Both of them are now dead, so Warren is short-handed and the ranch is without leadership. I think we need to have another long talk with Will Austin."

"You're thinking that Amos Warren might just get crazy and do something stupid?" Jack Slater gave his son a long look. "It would be like him." Jack tried to picture Amos Warren letting his anger get the best of him and actually attacking the Slater ranch. It was an ugly picture.

"I want to stop and talk with Rick Burdick in Skelton before heading home. He might have eyes on Amos Warren or at least have some idea of what's on the fat man's mind."

"You're just hoping that Burdick will be having a cold one with Horseface Hawkins, that's what you're thinkin'." Rob was laughing when Jack simply gave him a shrug.

They tied off in front of the Alabama House Saloon and found a busy crowd inside listening to old Doc Whitney carrying on.

"That fat old dog said he was ropin' critters for the branding fire and fell off his horse, his revolver fell out and hit a stone and fired off, sending a bullet into a hundred pounds of fat in his shoulder." He was cackling louder than Horseface Hawkins as he told the tale and half of Skelton, in for an afternoon's cold beer, were right with him.

"I thought doctors weren't supposed to be

telling tales about their patients, Doc? Is this different?" Hoseface asked.

"When it's a bald faced lie like this one, it's more than different," Doc Whitney said. "Amos Warren did something wrong is all I can tell you."

"Looks like we got the punch line but missed the story," Jack Slater said. "Doc, you been drinkin' that hard stuff again?"

"Hey, Jack Slater. Haven't had a taste in years. Don't need to when I have people like Amos Warren to attend to. He ain't got the truth in him. He's a got a real hate for you."

"You said he shot himself accidentally?"

"No, I said that's what he told me," Whitney said. There was another round of laughter from the men at the bar. "The story I got from one of his men is considerably darker and meaner. He got in an argument with one of his hands, Jake Winters it was, whipped him bloody with his quirt and then shot him. Winters was the one who shot Warren as he was dyin'. Nasty business."

The atmosphere darkened when Doc told the real story and it was Jesse Winthrop who spoke up. "Winters was the Warren man that was here just a few days ago. He was with that feller that rode off after you, Jack."

"You mean Will Austin? Oh, dear. Austin ain't gonna like hearing this story. Winters was thinking of leaving Warren, too. I wonder if that's what provoked the killing? I was hoping to find Rick Burdick here. Anybody seen him?"

"I told him what I found out at Warren's place and he rode out to talk with Amos." Doc Whitney downed his beer and walked out, shaking his head. "Nasty times."

Jack and Rob finished their beer and rode for home. "Well, old son, we learned a few things on this little trip, eh?" Jack Slater had a tired smile on his face as they rode toward a quickly setting spring sun. "Learned how to pack frozen beef but not how to alter bills of sale. Learned how to sell beef to a packing house without having to provide ownership papers because as a feedlot you've already proven ownership."

"You're a fast learn, Dad." Rob Slater said. "Now all we have to do is have some lawman prove it."

"That and keep Amos Warren from burning us out. We better pick it up if we want to get home in time for supper." It was a full-out race between father and son on finely bred ranch horses that loved to run and the dust was flying as they reined in at the corrals, neck and neck the whole way.

"Whew!" Jack yelped, leaping from his horse and yelling it out again. "I love good horses."

"Better hurry, Dad. It looks like the crew are already in the house. I'll take care of the horses and our gear. I'm sure Mama heard us coming in."

16

Deputy Sheriff Rick Burdick wasn't five minutes out of town when he ran into Three-toes heading the other way. "Been at the Warren Ranch all day, Three-toes?" The buckaroo nodded. "Got a couple of questions to ask you. Got word your boss was shot and another man killed. What can you tell me about that?"

"Ain't nobody dead that I know of," Three-toes lied.

"And Warren?"

"Fell off his horse and shot himself. He's fine. Gotta go. Want to make Elko before dark."

"You coming back?" Burdick asked. He was having a hard time holding his temper knowing full well that Three-toes was lying straight out. "I'm riding out to visit Amos Warren now."

"Riding in to hire us some men is all," Three-toes said. He turned his horse and trotted off north. Burdick watched for a few moments and continued his ride to Warren's place, several miles south.

Might have to use the hard questions, he thought. *Doc said at least one man was killed by Warren and his gunshot wound could not possibly have happened as described. I think I'll start by looking for some fresh digging. Gotta get word to the sheriff as soon as I know something but I doubt if Peabody would know what to do.*

Burdick rode into the large yard separating the ranch house from the barns and corrals and tied his horse off at one of the corrals. A buckaroo was exercising a couple of colts and walked over. "Help you with something, Deputy?"

"Want to talk with Amos Warren. He up at the house? I don't think we've met. I'm Elko Deputy Rick Burdick. What's your name."

"Name's Delgado. Ricardo Delgado. Interesting, eh? Yeah, Warren's got a gunshot wound and is suffering at a table full of food at the moment."

Burdick had to laugh, caught Delgado holding in a chuckle. "Thanks. Heard there was some problems around here this morning. How'd the boss get shot?"

Delgado got a worried look on his face and stammered out something Burdick couldn't understand. "Slow it down, Delgado. Just come out with it." Delgado was more than nervous, was looking around to make sure no one was around. "It's just us, Delgado. Tell me what happened."

"Mr. Warren, well," and Delgado continued looking all around as quick as he could move his head and Burdick just stood right in front of him, separated by the corral rails.

"Go on, Delgado. Warren did what?"

"He whipped on old Jake Winters so bad. Man was bleeding terrible and then Mr. Warren, well, he shot him. Killed him, Deputy. Killed his own man."

"Did Winters provoke the beating?" Burdick asked, knowing from the doctor that he hadn't.

"No, no," Delgado said. "No. Winters brought Warren some information that brought on this terrible beating. Before old Jake died, he shot Mr. Warren but didn't kill him. Mr. Warren's got a terrible temper, Deputy."

"Where'd they stuff Jake Winters' body, Delgado? Just tell me, don't point in case someone is watching."

"There's a trash pile behind the tack barn. Mr. Warren made us move the trash and bury Jake, then move the trash back on top. Wouldn't even let us say words over the old man. I feel really bad about all this, Deputy. I gotta get away from here."

Burdick knew that if Warren found out Delgado had been talking with him that Delgado's life was surely in jeopardy. "I wouldn't hesitate, either, Mr. Delgado. Pack light and ride fast. Stop at Valley Paddock's store in Skelton and tell him I want you protected. He'll know what to do. Don't wait, Delgado, not with Warren's temper."

Rick Delgado was a fine cow man, knew his animals, knew good care, and knew he could get a job anywhere. His horse was tied off inside the corrals with the two colts and he nodded to Burdick, walked over and took his horse out of the corral. He was on the road to Skelton inside of thirty seconds.

Burdick had a smile on his face as he walked to the kitchen porch of the rambling ranch house and was surprised to find Amos Warren sound asleep in a rocking chair, an empty platter with the remains of his dinner on a side table. "Hate to wake you, Mr. Warren, but we need to talk about what went on around here earlier today."

Warren jumped awake, knocked his platter and cup to the floor, and settled down, seeing the deputy standing there. "Ain't nothing to talk about, Burdick. Don't recall inviting you to my place. Time now for you to get on off the Warren place. I had an accident and that's all you need to know. Now get going." He reached down the side of the rocker and Burdick was much faster.

Burdick's fully cocked Colt was aimed for Warren's left eye. "Nice and slow, Warren. Put the little popper on the floor next to the bone plate. No call for more spilled blood." He watched Amos Warren ease the Remington from the side of the rocker and placed it on the floor. "That was fine," Burdick said and picked the piece up. He spilled the live rounds onto the ground and laid the weapon back at Warren's feet.

"Now, about earlier today. Let's start with how you got shot and then we'll talk about other things."

"Ain't no other things, Burdick. I fell off my horse if you have to know and my gun went off. Ain't nothing else to tell about. Now, that's all. Go on somewhere else. You ain't welcome here."

"Where would I find Jake Winters. I would like to talk with the gentleman before I leave," Burdick said. Warren's face and body never changed when the name came up.

"Don't rightly know, Burdick. Man don't work here no more. Left out sometime yesterday or the day before. Got some money coming, so if you find him, let him know." Warren had a smug look on his fat face and reached inside his coat for a cigar. Burdick's Colt was in his face that fast.

"You can't really be that stupid, Deputy, that you would think I'd pull a gun on you a second time. Are you? Huh? No, can't be that stupid." Warren had to fight to keep his anger under control. He took his time lighting the cigar and watched as Burdick tucked the big sidearm away. Burdick smiled as he walked down off the porch. "Don't forget, Burdick. You ain't welcome here."

"There's a lot I won't forget, Mr. Warren. I won't forget you tried to pull on me once. I'll see you again soon." He rode off at a slow walk, staring at Warren the whole time and smiled when he turned away and nudged his horse into a comfortable trot. *Man's about as arrogant as I want to deal with. Hope the sheriff gets me a court order to search that trash pile. Fell off his horse? As fat as he is he couldn't get on a horse.*

The supper table at the Slater ranch was full that night as Jack and Rob told of what they found in Halleck. Cactus Jack Faraday was most interested when Rob went into detail on freezing and boxing the beef for transport. "When they move those boxes into the refrigerated rail cars they don't have to provide paperwork or ownership? Don't have to prove they had the right to process that beef?"

"That's about the size of it. If it cleared the feedlot, then the transfer to the packing house is automatic. The packing house is the owner and distributor. They're boxed by animal parts, Cactus. All sirloin, all shoulder and so forth. Many different animals in every crate."

Rob was still frowning from having to talk about Skinny Forbes and his show of stupidity at the saloon that first night. "Clearing up the rustling around these parts is going to be a lot harder than chasing some men on horseback. Once the stolen cattle are accepted by the feedlot, we lose them."

"So that's how Sonny Belafleur and those others were able to get rid of the cattle they stole?" Will Austin said. "Shouldn't it be time to call in the law?"

"I think there's just a whole lot more to it, Will." Jack Slater sat back and looked around the table. Most of his crew was there. Rob, Cactus Jack, Will Austin, Two-dog Sorenson, Pete Forest, Tiny Howard, and Tubs Paddock had put away more than fifteen pounds of roast beef, and were learning how new technology was being used by outlaws.

"They still gotta steal 'em, still gotta run 'em off, but after that, the whole picture of cattle rustling has changed," Rob said.

"I don't think it was Belafleur's operation," Jack said. "He was working for someone else and it wasn't Amos Warren. Warren isn't smart enough for this kind of operation. Don't get me wrong, Warren's involved some way, just not anywhere near the top rungs. I think this Blake Wilson character is fully involved, top to bottom."

"How do you prove something like that?" Cactus Jack asked. "If there's no paperwork from the feedlot forward, how do you prove anything?"

"Got me," Slater laughed. "That might be the hardest job yet and it certainly isn't one of our jobs. As Mr. Austin just said, it's time for the law to take over. Our job is not to let any of our beef anywhere near those feedlots." There was general laughter around the table, broken up by loud knocking on the kitchen door.

"I'll get it," Mims said. Jack jumped to his feet and held her back. He motioned for her to stand back and went to the door himself. Cactus Jack whirled around and stood on the other side of the door, pistol in hand. Rob simply unholstered his weapon and held it ready.

"Valley Paddock," Slater exclaimed. "What brings you all the way out here, this time of night."

"Got somebody with me you need to meet. Come on Rick, come on in."

17

"That's an amazing story, Delgado. And you told this to Rick Burdick?" Jack Slater and the crew sat in absolute silence as Ricardo Delgado spelled out what had taken place at the Warren ranch. Slater looked at Will Austin and saw fierce anger in the man's eyes. *This Will Austin is a man with deep feelings, I think. How could Amos Warren have done such a thing?*

"Will, is this even possible? I've known Warren to bluster, but has he shown this kind of abusive behavior and anger? These are the signs of a mad man. No one stands up to him?"

"No doubt about it, Jack. Warren has a terrible temper and has whipped and run off more than one hand with that quirt of his." Austin looked at Delgado, frowning. "Jake was a friend of mine, Rick. You say he was whipped and shot because he told Warren about me leaving? I'm gonna kill that fat slob."

"No, Will. Let's let the law handle this." Jack Slater looked around the table and saw more than one head nodding in agreement with Austin. Would some of his men join Austin, ride out and seek revenge? It was difficult for a man like Slater to fathom what he just heard and not think retribution. How could a man treat his employees, his fellow man, that way?

"Warren has threatened to burn us out and now we hear this. We need to be even more aware than we usually are. Cactus, I want men on the herds around the clock. We've been a little lax in that regard with our fenced pastures and all. Fences haven't meant much to the rustlers, I'm sure they wouldn't mean a thing to Warren."

"Rob, I want men around the barns and home place around the clock. I know it's spring and calves need attending and I'll bring more hands on to help."

Jack took a deep breath and looked around the table to see what kind of reaction he would get from the men. Adding onto already busy times isn't always well accepted. He got nods and a smile or two and nodded back with a smile. "Good. We had a fine branding, this isn't the time to let some dirty worm destroy things." He motioned for more coffee and sat back in his chair.

"Valley, when you get back to Skelton I want you to find Rick Burdick and ask him to pay us a visit."

"I'll do that and let the town know to be on the watch, too. How far can something like this go?" He was shaking his head as he slipped out the door, not getting an answer.

Jack looked at Delgado, sitting quietly with a forlorn look on his face. He had watched a friend get horsewhipped and killed and did nothing and instead of going after Amos Warren, he had run away. He was a better man than this and felt deeply ashamed.

"I should have done something," he whispered. His eyes were downcast, his fists clenching and releasing in anger and frustration. "I'm sorry, Will."

"What are your plans, Delgado? Are you blaming yourself for the killing? I'm sure Burdick already told you not to leave the area. You have to know that word of you telling Burdick and all of us about what happened will bring Warren's men down on you like a lightning strike."

"Mr. Paddock has offered me a place with him, but I would be a big target in that little village. I just stood there with the rest of the crew and watched the beating and then the killing. I knew I would die if I stepped in. I was wrong, cowardly."

"With Warren's size, terrible anger," Jack said. He looked at Delgado's sad face. "I'm not sure what anyone would do in a situation like that."

"I'm a good cow man, Mr. Slater. Will, you can vouch for me?"

"I can Ricky. You're good with horses, cattle, fences, anything to do with a good ranch." Will Austin looked over to Jack. "He's a fine hand, Jack."

"Put your gear in the bunkhouse, Delgado. You'll be safer here than in town, but that might not be saying much," Slater said. "I think that's enough for tonight. gentlemen. My head hurts with everything we've learned." The chuckles indicated that many heads hurt.

As the group broke up and moved out of the kitchen, Cactus Jack picked a couple to be night riders, and Rob picked one to watch the building around the home place. "What's our next move, Dad? We can't just sit around and wait for Amos to strike and we sure can't ride to his place, even if only to talk."

"No, we have to let the law handle all of this, I'm afraid. What we've heard is criminal and it isn't up to us to seek justice. It is up to us to help the law and I intend to do that."

"Hopefully, Rick Burdick will come out tomorrow. Mossy Peabody's been a fair sheriff. A little too showy for my blood and Burdick does his job around Skelton, so the Amos Warren killing will be investigated. As far as Blake Wilson and the packing plant? That might be more than they can handle. Let's sleep on it, son, and we'll start fresh in the morning."

Slater was giving thought to riding over to Ted Wilsons place and talking about getting the cattlemen's group involved in the feedlot/packing house situation. Maybe even talk to the attorney general or the governor. There's a huge hole in the current situation, a hole big enough for fat steer to fall through.

"I can't picture any of our men simply standing by and watch a man get whipped and then shot." Rob was shaking his head, looking down on the floor. "Mr. Warren needs a good thrashing and it should come from one of his own hands."

Three-toes Jacobs didn't ride into Elko. He went east instead, to Wilson's feedlot to tell the boss what had happened. He rode straight through and was exhausted when he finally walked into the office of the feedlot. Blake Wilson heard him ride in and was at door.

Three-toes flopped down in a chair. "Warren killed one of his own hands," he wheezed. "Others have run off. Our people are scattered, Mr. Wilson. The few we have left."

"Slow down, Three-toes. Tell me what happened." Blake Wilson wasn't ready for more bad news. "Were our men involved? I have been against this marriage with Warren from the beginning."

"Warren went nuts when he found out one of his hands, not one of our people, had left him. He horse whipped the man, Blake, drew blood from the man's face with that quirt of his, and then shot him dead. Now, the sheriff is involved."

"How did the sheriff get involved if it happened on the Warren ranch?"

"Old Winters shot Warren before he died, the doc came out, and then the Skelton deputy. Warren's men probably told him what happened."

"I never did like Sonny Belafleur's idea of mingling our people with a rancher's. We will have to let the law take its course, Three-toes. Let Amos Warren hang for murder and probably have his ranch sold out from under him beforehand. That's his problem, not mine." Blake Wilson paced around the great room trying to put this new wrinkle into place. "You said you were sent to fetch hands?" Three-toes nodded.

"Then, go back to the ranch without any extra hands, tell him whatever you want. We're finished with Amos Warren, but it's important that you get our people out of there. Tell what's left of our crew to ride to Elko and we'll get word to them. For god's sake, don't bring 'em here."

He paced around the generous office, stopped twice to look out the window at the almost empty feed pens, and knew this would not just blow over. "We have got to disassociate from Warren," he snarled. He was more talking to himself than to Three-toes. "Sheriff will swarm all over that ranch." He looked at Three-toes. "You buried the body under a trash pile? Any way you could get it out of there before the sheriff's people find it?"

"The deputy I talked to leaving out seemed to know that someone was killed. Don't have any idea what Warren might have said, though. I can't get back to the ranch until late tomorrow at the best, Mr. Wilson. Maybe I can find Odie and Skinny and get some help."

"Skinny's busy right now, Three-toes, and Odie Jackson is no longer part of the organization." Three-toes couldn't believe that. He just stood in the middle of the room, shaking his head. "You and Louie Bloom are the only ones left at the Warren place. Do your best, but try not to get involved if the sheriff's people are already on the job." He continued pacing around as Three-toes made his way out.

From a large crew to almost nobody and now killings. It's the one thing the law simply will not turn away from, the one thing I tried to make Sonny Belafleur understand. He never should have gotten so tight with Warren. He spent the next half hour writing down names on a piece of paper and one at a time, either marking them with a star or running a line through them.

He ended up with five starred names and called for Ling Ho. "We need to get word to these men to be here within three days. Use the telegraph office in Wells, not the one here in Halleck. We may have to talk about using your special skills when you get back. Hurry, now."

All five had worked more than one scheme with Blake Wilson in the past and were known criminals with paper hanging in various towns and cities. They were not known as killers or rustlers. Blake Wilson had enough of those types. These men got things done without seeming to get personally involved. *I've got to put a lid on this and the quicker I do it the better. Somebody's going to start seeing my connection to these Warren people who keep coming up dead and wounded. It all rolls back on Belafleur and bad decisions.* It never seemed to occur to the man that it was he who hired Belafleur.

Blake Wilson took a long walk through the holding pens of the feedlot, angry as a hungry wolf at the emptiness. "Anybody seen or heard from Skinny Forbes?" He asked his skeleton crew as they ate their mid-day dinner.

"Left out a couple of days ago, boss. Ain't seen him since. He buying cattle for us?"

"That's what I'm hoping." Blake Wilson never told his feedlot or packing house crews how the cattle came to be there. They had been introduced to him as a cattle broker from Denver with good knowledge of the business. It wasn't unusual for cattle from several brands to show up, but always with the proper paperwork. He had contracts for packaged beef from distributors in California, Oregon, and Nevada and his feedlots were all but empty.

That was why he knew he had to keep the law as far away from his operation as possible. Would that stupid fat rancher south of Skelton blow this money making operation up? That's all that was going through Blake Wilson's mind. How to stop that? How to eliminate Warren without bringing more lawmen into the picture? It was also a terrible time for him to lose the skills of Odie Jackson.

Duke Winters was getting settled in his new position of yard boss at the Elko Livestock, Auction, and Feedlot when he spotted Odie Jackson prowling around the feed pens. "You've got no business here, Jackson. You're on private property."

"I come looking for you, Duke." Jackson had a big smile on his face and walked his horse right up to Duke, offering his hand. "Thought maybe you'd like to go to work for me. Be moving cattle on a regular basis if my wires are answered. Good money in it for you."

Duke Winston knew Odie Jackson as one of the buyers that Blake Wilson used, never did get along with the man, and couldn't help remembering his last encounter at the saloon in Halleck. What kind of man is this? Winston could almost still see young Rob Slater with a gun to Jackson's head and now the man offers him a job?

"You've never had money before, Jackson, why would you have money now? Move cattle? Whose cattle?" Duke Winston knew that Jackson was around Blake Wilson's feedlot often, but didn't work there and always wondered if the association was more than just that of a buyer, a supplier. He and Skinny Forbes were always in a huddle with Wilson. He also remembered the quickness Jackson had with a knife and was waiting for the man to pull some stupid stunt or another.

"Better leave out before Art Simpson sees you. He ain't got no kind words for Blake Wilson or the men who ride for him." Duke nudged his horse around the end of a fence line to confront the outlaw and saw that Odie Jackson already had a large and shiny knife in his hand.

"You get more and more handy with your knives, don't you? Last time I saw you, I saw a knife taken away from you. Better leave while you can, Jackson." Winston was carrying a three foot section of rake handle with a cattle hook on the end of it.

"You want this hook through your heart, your liver, or your kidneys, Mr. Jackson? Your choice." He made a short lunge forward with the hook threatening and poised to strike. It was a vicious weapon, the pointed hook, meant to simply prod a stubborn cow, could rip and gash a man.

That shiny hook put fear in Jackson's face, something that hadn't been seen in a long time. One quick lunge and it would rip into a man's body, gouge out sensitive organs, and a man would face a lingering death.

"You'll regret this, Winston. I was offering something you won't see working here." He tucked the knife away and slowly turned away and walked his horse out of the feedlot. Duke Winters followed along, slowly, until Jackson was off the property.

"Who was that?" Art Simpson stepped out of the little office that fronted the feedlot operation. "Looks familiar."

"He used to hang around Blake Wilson's operation. Name's Odie Jackson. Caught him nosing around and ushered him off the place. Hope that's all right with you."

"More than all right, Mr. Winston," Simpson chuckled. "Anyone having dealings with Wilson has no business around here. That prod you're carrying have anything to do with his leaving in a hurry?"

"Works getting the cattle moving," Duke chuckled. "Jackson hung around with a man named Skinny Forbes. Wilson always said they were buyers and they would bring small groups of beef to the feedlot. Often. Mean anything to you?"

"No. I know there are buyers that operate in California and Colorado, but I buy right from the rancher. Shorty Watson will call for another fifty head in the next day or two. That packing house is busy this time of year. Can we fill his order?"

Watson had the packing house next door to the feedlot and shipped boxed and frozen beef west regularly. "That California market is huge, I guess." Simpson had run a small ranch in earlier years, but got into the feedlot business following an injury. "Ranchers are still shipping live cattle to the Stockton feedlots and what I've heard, Stockton can't keep up with demand."

"Our pens are filled nicely, sir," Winston said. "We can fill his order."

"What have you heard about these cattle that are being stolen around the county?" Simpson asked. "Ted Wilson seems to think Blake Wilson might be involved."

"So does Jack Slater down near Skelton. What I saw at Wilson's place, the cattle coming in all had legitimate bills of sale, so I don't know. Nothing seems out of the ordinary." Winston said. He watched Simpson head back into his office and he wandered back through the pens, figuring how to sort an order for Watson. He couldn't get Odie Jackson out of his mind.

Just what did that man have on his mind? Make a lot of money going to work for him? More than likely end up in prison. I wonder if some of those beeves coming into Wilson's place were stolen? Jackson worked hand in hand with Skinny Forbes and that fellow who was killed at the cattleman's dinner. Sonny Belafleur.

"Good morning, Jack. Nice to see you again." Mossy Peabody was stepping down from his lathered horse. "Got some nasty business to take care of, thought you might be interested in knowing about it."

"You're always welcome here, Sheriff. Come on in, we're sure to have hot coffee and maybe even a sweet roll or two." They walked across the large yard between the barns and the house. "If you're talking about a possible murder at Amos Warren's, I think I may know a couple of things."

"Would he kill one of his own men? Doesn't sound right." Peabody followed Jack into the big kitchen and found a chair. "Understand you have a man here who may have witnessed it, though."

"Ricardo Delgado is working for me now and he told us what happened. I think he told your deputy, Rick Burdick, too. What are your plans?"

"After I have a short talk with you and Delgado, Burdick and I are riding out to Warren's. I heard the body might be under a trash pile. It'll be a mess by now."

"Just the two of you? Warren hires men handy with their guns, Sheriff. I'd take a little backup if I were you."

"You offering?" Peabody chuckled.

"That would start a war immediately." Jack was laughing as he poured the two of them some more coffee. "No, you need men with you, though. I want to bend your ear on Blake Wilson before you get out of our valley. I think it's all connected, too."

"I've heard many stories, Jack, about Warren's men being seen around Blake Wilson's operation. Don't really have a handle on anything, though. I'd like Delgado to ride with me and Burdick. Can you spare him?"

"I can, but I mean it when I say you should have some backup."

"Amos might have a bloody temper but he ain't dumb enough to shoot the sheriff, Jack. We'll be fine." Peabody got up and walked to the door. "Let's find Delgado."

"You say you've heard stories about Blake Wilson. They have anything to do with stolen cattle?" Jack asked.

"More than one rancher has had their herds come up short and made complaints, suggesting that Blake Wilson had their cattle. I've never found any stolen cattle at his operation. I think it's just rumors and I'm not really that sure of the ranchers and their counting methods." The sheriff looked Jack right in the eye. "Are you suggesting something?"

"I don't have anything that could be taken to court, just ideas, Sheriff. After you leave Warren's place, or sometime soon, I'd like you to have a talk with my son. Rob probably knows as much or more about the feedlot and packing facility business than Blake Wilson and has some ideas you might be interested in."

"When he gets a chance, ask him to come on in to the office and we'll chat some. There's Delgado. Gotta go, Jack."

"Be safe, Sheriff and keep my new man safe." He stood near a corral fence and watched them ride out. *That man's got a lot of faith in himself and I've got none right at the moment. Naive to a fault. Burdick and Delgado are riding with a man who doesn't believe he can be hurt.*

18

"If he tries to use that whip on me, I'll gun him down, Sheriff. I mean it. He's quick and mean with that thing. More than one man can back that up." Delgado was sure that he was ready to ride back to the Warren ranch with the sheriff, but wanted assurances that he would be leaving again, too. For several days he'd been wrapped in anger with how he let Warren whip on a fellow cow man, and then shoot him dead. The fact he just sat on the fence and watched was almost more than the man could handle.

"You'll be under our protection, Ricardo," Burdick said. "Warren is sure to try something, particularly since he knows you were standing at the corral when the beating and killing took place. You probably won't have to say anything."

"He's a fat old man, Mr. Delgado. He might have a whip, maybe even a gun, but he's still a fat old man who can't move faster than any of us," Sheriff

Peabody said. "Just don't be starting something, let Deputy Burdick and I handle this."

Don't start something? Delgado was shaking his head. *Just let that fat old man make one wrong move and you'll see this buckaroo start something.* Revenge had flowed with the blood in his body and Delgado was almost praying that Amos Warren would start something. *There will be no more standing by and watching.* It was a simple declaration, deceptively simple.

The ride south was fast and the three trotted right up to the hitching rack at the back of the house. Amos Warren was sitting in his rocker, a platter of sweet rolls on the table next to him. "You're on private property, Sheriff. You can turn those horses right around and ride off."

"Here on business, Warren. Official and nasty business," Mossy Peabody said. The three stepped off their horses without waiting for the traditional invite and walked right up onto the porch. Peabody stood in front of the hefty rancher and leaned up against the porch railing.

"That story you told Deputy Burdick wasn't the truth, now, was it, Mr. Warren." It was not a question and Warren didn't flinch or indicate he even heard the sheriff. "You were shot by one of your own hands, weren't you?"

"You calling me a liar, Peabody?" Amos Warren

all but jumped from the rocking chair, knocking the table over, scattering sweet rolls and the now broken platter about. He wasn't wearing a sidearm but grabbed for the quirt, which was next to the chair.

"No, no," Burdick said. He pulled his revolver but the fat old man was much faster and Burdick felt the sting of the quirt knocking the gun from his hand. Before Warren could make another slash at the deputy or sheriff, Ricardo Delgado leaped at the rancher the two of them breaking through the railing and falling three feet off the porch into rocks.

Peabody was stunned at how fast Warren was able to move and hesitated just moments before he leaped off the porch. He had his pistol in hand and hit Warren twice before he could slash at Delgado. Two rifle shots came from the barn and Delgado fell, a bullet through the middle of his back. The other bullet slammed into the rocks, spattering them onto the sheriff. Peabody rolled toward Warren and used him as a shield as other rounds were fired from the barn.

"You all right, Sheriff?" Burdick yelled, trying to hide behind the overturned table and rocking chair. "Just one shooter, I think."

"Keep him busy for a minute," Peabody yelled. Burdick started firing his revolver quickly at the open barn doors and Peabody made a dash off to the side and away from the house. He dodged through farm machinery, wagons, and assorted equipment, getting to the corrals without any return fire.

Should have brought more men with me, should have had Burdick check the barn. He had a head full of should haves. *Should have had my pistol in my hand talking to that man. Should have listened to Jack Slater.*

"Should have brought my rifle," he murmured right out loud. It was a hard crawl through dust and dirt, road apples, and tobacco juice, to the side of the barn. He signaled Burdick to keep shooting and slowly made his way to a window at the side of the barn where he could see inside. One man was next to the open door, reloading his rifle.

Peabody moved toward the sliding doors and waved to Burdick to quit shooting. He stepped into the opening and unloaded three fast shots into Louie Bloom's body before the man even knew he was there. Burdick came running. "Any more?"

"Hope not," Peabody said. "Know this man? Work for Warren does he?"

"Name's Bloom. Louie Bloom. Worked more for Sonny Belafleur than Amos Warren. Ricky Delgado's dead and Warren's starting to come to. I'll go back and take care of him."

"Put him in irons before you do anything. I've never seen a man of his size move that fast." Peabody dragged Bloom's body over to where Burdick was starting on Warren.

"Busted his gunshot wound loose, Sheriff. Got a busted leg, too. We need some help. Warren needs a doc and with this heat, we've gotta take care of these dead men."

"I'm gonna have a hard time with this one, Rick. I told Delgado, as we rode in here, that I would protect him. Ain't much of a sheriff sometimes. We got us a mess to clean up." *I'm not going to run for re-election, not after this. Two dead men right here, one wounded badly and if I had done my job there wouldn't be any.*

"Let's move Warren into the house and you do what you can. I'll move the dead ones into the barn and start working on graves." Peabody knew he was wrong in not bringing men with him, knew he would face the wrath of the public when they found out. The least he could do was tend the dead.

Three-toes Jacobs was about a half mile from the Warren ranch when he heard a series of gunshots and pulled up quick. "Too late. Too bad, Mr. Warren." He turned his horse and made a quick run to Skelton where he sent a wire to Blake Wilson. It would be hours before Wilson got it delivered and he knew he couldn't wait around in that town.

Three-toes was on the road to Elko in minutes wondering just how much the sheriff might find out. *Was there any kind of paper work? From*

Sonny? From Amos? Should I run for Halleck and the feed lot? Or head for Reno or Virginia City? He decided to ride for the feedlot, let Wilson know everything that he knew, and then make a decision. *I can always take the train to Salt Lake and head north into Wyoming country.*

"We had such a good thing going, too," he muttered. "Take just a few steers at a time, Blake Wilson always said, but it was Sonny Belafleur who got all selfish, wanting more, always more. All that gone now."

He rode in silence the rest of the way to the main road east, spent the night in a warm little camp under some cottonwood trees, and made serious plans. "I can't go anywhere with empty pockets and no provisions, so that needs to be answered before anything and the answer is Blake Wilson. That man does have money and I know where he keeps it. I'm gonna get my pockets filled with it."

The one sided conversation continued well into the night and when morning came, Three-toes was on the road with a plan. Blake Wilson would not like what those plans included.

"Before I get started, Rick," the sheriff said, helping him get Warren into the house. "I need a list of names of people that should be here at this ranch. Then, I need to get back to Skelton and send out wires to all the resident deputies in the county to be on the lookout for those men. Hurry with that list." Sheriff Peabody was in the kitchen of Warren's ranch house with Burdick and Warren's cook.

"Get me some blankets, Cookie," Peabody said. "I need to take care of these bodies before it gets hot." Burdick sat at the table and wrote a quick list of the men he knew worked for Warren.

"I'll get them buried and then find Jake Winters body," Burdick said. "Don't think either one of us expected this, Sheriff."

"Can't get Delgado out of my mind, Burdick. I was warned by Jack Slater and I let that man Delgado down."

"I don't think he would see it that way, Sheriff. He jumped Warren. He was working for you, protecting us. No, Sheriff, you didn't let him down. He did the right thing and it cost him."

Peabody shook his head, took the list, and walked out of the kitchen without another word. "I'll send the doc." He rode as quick as he dared back to Skelton. He made a quick stop at Doc Whitney's and rode fast to the telegraph office.

Burdick had Warren's bleeding wounds covered and had him tied to the bed. "Sleep tight you murdering fool. I'm going to bury a good man who didn't deserve to die and then I'm going to testify that it was your fault. You'll hang, fat man."

"Busy place around here, today," Squeaky Mc-Farland said. Her bright green eyes were dancing with pleasure. "I can go days without sending or getting a wire and here, we have two men sending wires all over."

"Oh?" Peabody looked at the tiny lady sitting at the desk. "Who might this other person have been?"

"Ain't supposed to tell that, Sheriff. Not even to a sheriff."

"If I pull my pistol, cock it, and place it up your pretty little nose, you'd surely tell me, wouldn't you?" As far as she could see the sheriff was not smiling and his hand was moving slowly toward that big gun on his waist.

"It was Three-toes Jacobs, sir." She just blurted it out. She was actually shaking in fear and Peabody had to laugh. She handed him a copy of what Three-toes sent. "That wasn't funny, Sheriff. Would you really do that?"

"I would never do that to such a lovely lady and fine upstanding citizen," he said. He held the wire up and read it quickly. "So, Blake Wilson's back in the picture." The conversation with Jack flashed through his mind. "I wonder just how much Slater really knows." Peabody wrote out what the telegrams should say to all the little towns and villages in the county for the resident deputies to be on the watch for Three-toes Jacobs, Odie Jackson, and Skinny Forbes.

"Thank you for not letting me shoot you, Squeaky." Mossy Peabody smiled and handed the lady a silver dollar. "I'd really miss that pretty smile of yours. If Rick Burdick comes in, tell him I'll be at the Slater ranch." She couldn't hold back the little giggle and tapped out Peabody's wires, sending them on their way.

Peabody rode back over to Doc Whitney's place and told him about the fracas at the Warren place. "I have to get out to Slater's place and Burdick is alone at Warren's. Can you get Valley Paddock or some of the men to accompany you out there?" *Slater was far more right than he'll ever know. All I had to do was listen. Just listen. Something I have a hard time with.*

"I'll head out right now, Sheriff. You said the old wound is open and bleeding. Good," he snickered. "Now, a broken arm, too. Good. I might be a doctor, a fine one, if I say so myself, but there are some men who just need to be hurt and Amos Warren is one of them. I'll gather a good number to ride out with me." If he hadn't chosen medicine for a career, Whitney surely would have been a lawman.

"It was nasty, Jack." The sheriff and Jack Slater were walking through the barn on a hot spring afternoon. "I should have listened to you, Jack.

You were right and that fat old man had me at his mercy, of which, he showed none." Peabody stopped and kicked some dirt.

"Ricardo Delgado was a true hero, but it cost him dearly. Amos acted in raw, naked anger and the man, Bloom, Louie Bloom died supporting him." He reached in his pocket for his list. "What do you know of these men, Three-toes Jacobs, Odie Jackson, and Skinny Forbes? Burdick seems to think they worked for Sonny Belafleur instead of Amos Warren."

"It's a hard question to answer, Sheriff. Belafleur worked for Warren, but many of the men who rode with Belafleur weren't on the Warren payroll. Rob and I ran into Odie Jackson in Halleck and he called himself a Blake Wilson man. I think Belafleur was running a gang of cattle rustlers and selling the beeves to Blake Wilson."

"That's a mighty strong accusation, Jack. Do you have anything to back that up? Anything other than what you just suggested?"

"Not a thing, Sheriff, but you'll be the first to know when I do." Slater was fighting hard to hold his anger in. He wanted to say it's your responsibility to investigate, not mine. He wanted to say, Why didn't you take men with you? When an innocent man is killed and it's something you warned the sheriff about, it's almost impossible to be quiet.

Peabody took a long look at Jack Slater. *So, he's injecting himself into what should be my investigation. Just what does he know? And if he does know something, why does he know it? Warren's been after Slater for years but never took any stupid chances or made any really dumb moves until recently.* Peabody then recognized that 'recently' meant following Sonny Belafleur's going to work for Warren. *The rustling started not too long after Belafleur joined Warren, too. Slater's putting all this together and I'm not.*

"According to Squeaky at the telegraph office, Three-toes sent a wire to Blake Wilson earlier today saying I had raided the Warren ranch and there was shooting. You might be right that Belafleur worked for Wilson."

"You need to get some information on Wilson's businesses. I wanted you to talk to Rob about this but he's out with Cactus Jack moving calves today." Jack sat back in his chair and took a sip of coffee. *Rob could do this so much better than me but the sheriff needs to know this stuff now. If those Warren men were the rustlers and they were selling to Wilson, Peabody needs to know that now.*

"From what I know, Sheriff, if a steer comes to Blake Wilson's feedlot with all the legal papers, he can then move it to the packing plant and the packing plant can ship it without further proof of ownership. The law favors Wilson's operation."

"You seem awfully well informed on this," Peabody said. Jack saw some of his own original questions splashed across Peabody's face and had to gently chuckle.

"Not me, Sheriff. My son, Robbie, has been studying these new processes, has a working knowledge of feedlots and packing houses, transportation of frozen carcasses and boxed sections, and how the laws are written. Talk to him and you'll know probably more than Blake Wilson."

"I wanted to head back to Elko right away but you've got me all fired up now. Let's ride out and find your son. Missing cattle, dead men in several locations, and Blake Wilson's name continually coming up. I ain't much of a sheriff, Jack, but I am trying."

Jack was laughing gently as they walked from the kitchen and headed for their horses. "Rob's in the north section and we could use a nice ride on a hot afternoon. Hope you're ready to learn about what life is going to be like in the twentieth century. Rob seems to think mechanical devices will replace human beings in most of the work force."

"We've still got a few years left of this one, Jack. I don't think I want to be ready. What does he mean, mechanical devices?"

"You've seen pictures of those monster steam traction engines they're using back east. They look like railroad engines on wheels. Not for me," Jack said. "Now they're making other machines to carry people. They'll never replace a horse, Sheriff."

Jack was contemplative as they rode through deep sage, fresh grass, and warm temperatures. "I've never been afraid of the future, Sheriff. Not ever. But I wonder if we are really ready for what my son keeps yapping about? I grew up with railroads, but using a railroad engine to plow your ground?"

"I've spent more winter mornings cutting ice and moving it to ice houses for summer's use than you can imagine. But creating ice in the middle of summer? Using some kind of machinery? And shipping carcasses, for days on end, across the country without the meat rotting? No, Sheriff, I'm not looking forward to this new century racing its way toward us."

19

Skinny Forbes was in a valley near Mary's River, moving seven steers he had rounded up the night before. He grumbled all night as he worked over hot coals, altering the brands such that they matched the bills of sale he had in his pocket. "Too easy," he said. He was changing bar W to cross W. He knew he was going after bar W cattle and Blake had the bills of sale already made up for cross W cattle. It was the gathering that had him angry and out of sorts.

It was far more of a job than one man should have to do and he cussed out Belafleur for dying, cussed out Odie Jackson for riding off, and cussed out Blake Wilson for hiring them. It was times like this that he wondered what he was thinking when Blake Wilson invited him to come to Nevada with him. Robbing banks in Colorado, Kansas, Nebraska, and Oklahoma was so much easier to do.

"On the other hand," he snickered, "I ain't been shot at in a long time." Moving the small herd all the night long brought him almost back to the feedlot. "I'm gonna have to have a talk with that man." He was muttering, planning how he would talk it out and time moved by quickly. "I'll just lay it out to him, bring in more men or do all of this yourself. That's what I'll do and get out of this country."

He was following a single track trail that led from a ridge, down two miles to the feedlot. "Ain't the time to be short-handed." He said it right out. "Could have had another ten or more calves if I had some help. Gonna tell Wilson, too."

He knew Blake Wilson would throw a fit at getting only seven steers, but without other men, that's all he could put together. Getting the running irons right, the branding done. and the papers filled out all the while keeping the little herd together was almost too much for one man. *I don't know who I want to shoot the most. Sonny's dead or he would be first. Odie needs to die, and Wilson needs to be hurt bad. My cut on this better be good.*

Just as if he were a rancher bringing his stock to the feedlot, Forbes would be paid by the weight of the animals. It would be less than market value, though. Wilson would often add a little of what he called, an incentive bonus. Skinny drove the cattle to the loading pen where the brands were checked by one of the feedlot workers and the bills of sale were recorded. All the paperwork was done faithfully with every bunch that was brought in.

The inspection was cursory at best since the laws themselves were rather vague. It was general practice that the ranchers involved did the serious inspections. The idea of brand inspectors had not reached Nevada. In Elko County, the branding rules dated back to 1873 and the county recorder kept the records. As long as the seller had either bills of sale for the cattle or claimed they were carrying his brand, the feedlot would make the buy.

"Mr. Wilson in the office?" Skinny Forbes asked, getting the receipts. "I'll take these in for you. Kind of in a hurry today." He was always friendly with the workers, unlike Jackson and they would bend some of the already loose rules for him if he asked. Those working the feedlots and the packing house had no idea they were dealing in stolen beef.

"He's there," one said. "Been asking if we've seen you."

Forbes put his horse up and was walking toward the office when he saw a rider coming down the siding. "Well, Three-toes, what brings you all the way out here. Get enough of that fat old Amos Warren?"

"Warren's dead, I think, Skinny. Jake's dead, Willard's run off, and you and me are what's left. Sent a wire to Wilson. Didn't he tell you?"

"Just got here myself, Three-toes. Gonna be one upset man, I'm afraid." They walked the short distance from the feed pens to the office. Ling Ho had a grave look on his face when they walked in. He shook his head as if to say, 'don't go in there,' but they went anyway.

"Morning, Blake. Here are the receipts. Couldn't get any more and still get 'em here. Three-toes just told me about Warren."

"Don't give a hoot about Warren, Skinny, but what I've got right now bothers me. It's just us three and empty feed pens out there. I've got standing contracts in California, Nevada, and Utah, Skinny. We need full pens out there. I got word this morning that Henry Wheeler is bringing two of his men in from Colorado this week. You ever work with him?"

"Most dangerous man I ever worked with, Blake." Forbes wasn't smiling. "Killed a man cuz the coffee got cold one morning, down on the Pecos, if I recall. He's good with runnin' irons, though."

"Don't care none about rules," Three-toes said. "He'll do it his way no matter how you want it done. He's just another Sonny Belafleur in my mind."

Blake Wilson had to laugh about the coffee incident but got serious again immediately. "Find us several areas close by where we can run ten or twelve calves in here quick-like when he gets here. Two or three times, bring in ten or twelve at a time. Something like that close by?"

"There is some fine pickin's in the Star Valley, south of Deeth, Blake. Me and Three-toes can have some steers put up and branded in brush pens before they get here."

Skinny Forbes found himself caught up in the news of Wheeler coming on board and all his late night talks with himself disappeared. "I was north of there, along Mary's River with these I brought in this morning and there are more up that way, too."

"Good. Skinny. I want you and Wheeler to work together on this. They'll be his men, so don't get him all riled up." Blake Wilson looked into Skinny Forbes' eyes and saw many questions that he would not be answering. "You all right with that?"

"I'm not one of Wheeler's men, Blake. I work for you. If you want me to work with Wheeler, I will, but I won't work for Wheeler. He needs to know that and if you don't make it clear, I will."

"That's all I'm asking, Skinny, that you work with Henry Wheeler. How about you, Three-toes?"

"Like Skinny, I work for you." He let it drop without further comment, but knew that some-day soon, he would light out and get away from what was becoming far too dangerous for his blood. Maybe take Blake Wilson out, too. *I kind of thought all along that this little operation of his seemed too easy. He can't see it falling apart but I can. I can see that safe full of money, too. And, now we get to work with Henry Wheeler.*

While Blake Wilson laid out some more plans, Three-toes spent time looking, furtively as he could, to find the large safe he knew was in that room. He still had strong thoughts of killing Blake Wilson, taking what money was available, and leaving out. There was a curtain hanging behind a large sofa but no window behind it. *Gotcha, Blake Wilson.*

Three-toes and Skinny walked out of the office together. "Don't like the idea of working with Wheeler," Forbes said. "Dangerous man."

"I'll make a run or two with him, but I've got other plans," Three-toes said. "I've had as much of Blake Wilson as I can take. Most of those dead men were my friends and it's because of Wilson trusting Sonny Belafleur that they're dead."

"Don't leave me hanging, Three-toes."

"Wouldn't do that, Skinny. It's us against Wheeler and I plan to live through it."

Wheeler stood slightly less than five feet and ten inches and weighed about a hundred and fifty pounds. Wiry and strong, amoral at best, and with a terrible temper. He swung on board the train as it started moving out from Cheyenne and wandered through the coaches until he found Clint

Sloan and Beer Belly Bunker. "Glad you could make it, Sloan. How you feeling, Beer Belly?"

"All healed up, Boss," Bunker said. "You really planning on doing something for that snake Wilson? He ain't right in the head, Henry." Beer Belly Bunker was a huge man, could drink half a barrel of beer and still draw and shoot straight, walk tall, and speak clear. "He done us wrong that last time."

Bunker spent considerable time working for himself instead of running full time with Wheeler. He enjoyed jumping stage coaches on short hauls where the railroads couldn't go. He also hit the small banks, gambling halls, even lowering his standards to rob small merchants. He got shot up bad on his last attempt at a small town bank in eastern Colorado. "I'm healed up fine, Wheeler, but I still don't trust Wilson."

"He's got himself a nice little operation that will make us rich, Bunker, my man. We'll eat his beef, drink his whiskey, and take his money." He laughed loud and whopped Bunker across the shoulders. "Here's his deal and it fits us nice."

Henry Wheeler laid out Blake Wilson's operation for the men as they passed a bottle around. "Only thing I don't like about it is we will have to work with a couple of Wilson's men. One, Skinny Forbes, will shoot you down if you mess with him. The other, they call him Three-toes Jacobs, I've worked with him before. Three-toes is all right."

"I'd just as soon shoot Skinny Forbes when we get there," Clint Sloan said. "Him and his brother Toby cut me and my boys out of a deal down in Texas a while back. Cost me a fortune and a friend."

"Wait until we get the money, Clint," Wheeler said. "Then, do whatever you want."

"You're not planning to work with Wilson a bit, are you?" Beer Belly Bunker was almost laughing. "We're gonna take what the man has in his safe, aren't we?"

"You are quick, Mr. Bunker." Wheeler reached inside his jacket and pulled out two telegrams. "I got these on the same day, boys. One is from Wilson offering us the deal I've been telling you about. The other is from an old friend. I wasn't going to bring it up until we had a chance to talk to him, but his deal is much better, if he's right. We'll know, not long after we reach Elko."

The train pulled into Elko late in the day and the men retrieved their horses and packs. "I thought we were supposed to be meeting Wilson in Halleck. We went right on by, Henry." Sloan said.

"Wilson doesn't want us to be known in that burg. There's a small sleeping hotel called the Weeping Widow, got a saloon next door, where we'll meet up with my old friend. On the other side of the tracks and east some." They rode out, found the place and got ready to settle in.

"Should have just made us a camp somewhere, Henry. This is filthy." They were standing in what passed for a lobby looking at a haggard woman in her late fifties. There were shreds of carpet left on the floor and the hallway leading to rooms was dark as night. Clint Sloan couldn't see a lamp anywhere in the room. "Not for me, Henry."

"You Wheeler?" The old woman asked in a whiskey and cigar throat voice. Wheeler nodded. "Man waitin' for you in room two. Fifty cents please."

"Maybe later, woman, after we talk with the man in room two." He led the men down the dark hallway, found room two, and banged on the door.

"You in there. There are three guns coming in."

"Ha ha," a voice laughed. "Henry Wheeler and company, here at last. Come on in."

20

"You had to work hard to find a place this filthy to meet, Jackson. We ain't staying here," Wheeler said. "I hope this plan of yours has more thought to it than picking this place shows. I had good thoughts about your plan until we walked in here. Better start talking fast, Odie, or we're walking right out the door."

Henry Wheeler had swaggered down the filthy corridor, letting his anger build with every step and Beer Belly Bunker simply showed his disdain with a well-placed wad of tobacco juice. Wheeler and his men were glaring at Jackson and it was evident that after nearly a thousand miles in noisy railcars they were not to be toyed with.

"We are walking right out the door, gentlemen. Figured nobody would see you coming here and as soon as it gets dark we'll ride east to much better accommodations. Seems there are people asking questions about Blake Wilson's operation and the less anyone knows about us being together, the better. Have a drink," he said.

Wheeler calmed down and the four men sat in the filthy room for several hours talking about how best to take out Blake Wilson and the fortune he had stashed in the safe in his large office at the packing plant. "I've seen that safe open, Henry. He has stacks of currency, banded, inside. More than in any bank I've ever seen. It's just him and that Chinese cook of his at the place just about any night."

"I met Ling Ho," Beer Belly Bunker said. "He ain't just a Chinese cook, you know. He's a trained assassin. Had to flee China after an attempted uprising of some sort. That man doesn't need weapons but has them close at hand. Best not to simply write him off."

"Who else will we run into, Odie?" Henry Wheeler was getting second thoughts. It was supposed to be a simple hit and run. Shoot Wilson and the cook, take the money, and run. Now, Jackson has introduced a problem. "You holding things back from me? I don't like that, Jackson. I don't like that at all."

Wheeler was on his feet, fingers grasping and letting go of that killing machine at his hip, lacing about the cramped room. "Another change? Somebody looking to die? Gettin' mighty tired of all this."

Odie Jackson could feel the anger, knew Wheeler's temper, and started talking fast. "The feedlot crew, don't know anything about the rustling operation. They shouldn't get involved at all. Wilson only has Skinny Forbes and Three-toes Jacobs working the rustling operation now. Everyone else is dead or run off."

"Forbes, eh? Yeah, I know him." Wheeler calmed down a bit, even got a slight smile thinking of Skinny Forbes. "Hope he tries to pull down on me. I want to watch him die slow. Very slow. Anyone else?"

Jackson shook his head and the four men walked out of the hotel, mounted up and rode east, toward Halleck. Jackson left a silver dollar on the nightstand.

Robbie Slater spent several hours with Sheriff Mossy Peabody, riding back to the ranch and at the supper table. They were sitting in easy chairs before the fire with glasses of brandy. "That's about everything I know about the current situation with feedlots and packing houses, Sheriff. It's a whole new world from what you and my dad know. Because of what I've outlined to you, an entire set of new laws need to be written covering the gaps I've mentioned."

"Those aren't gaps, Rob. They're craters." Peabody laughed and took a long drink of brandy. "This Blake Wilson has himself pretty well shielded is what I'm seeing. I can't just ride up and accuse the man of buying rustled cattle or of hiring the rustlers, now, can I?"

"That's the problem, Sheriff. We are fairly sure it's happening, but how do you prove it? Catch the rustlers in the act and you stop the rustling only. Changing brands and having phony bills of sale to prove ownership, is quite another story. Dad and I are in the same boat as you, Sheriff. We would like to be able to help and have no idea how."

"You have given me some names, Rob and that's a big help. You also said that Will Austin was familiar with how Sonny Belafleur worked the rustling. I have an idea, but I'll need the full backing of your father. Can you get him in here?"

"He's in the barn with Cactus Jack and some of the men. Let's walk out there. Austin might be with them."

They found Jack and some of the crew sitting around a small fire outside the bunkhouse, enjoying some of Horseface Hawkins' good bourbon. "You two finally through jawin' up a storm?" Jack was on his haunches, stirring the fire. "I'll bet you know enough about the cattle business to open a school, by now, Sheriff."

"Just about," Peabody laughed. "With what Rob has told me, I think I might be able to put an end to all this. It will mean both him and Will Austin coming to work for me for a while. You up to that, Slater?"

"You're talking about running off with my cow boss and my new buckaroo? Just as spring gets ready to turn into summer? That's a mighty big question, Sheriff." Jack looked over to where Rob was sitting with Cactus Jack Faraday and shook his head. "This isn't the time to lose Rob. He and Cactus Jack are the two most important men on this ranch. You're askin' too much, Mossy."

The man's got a whole department of deputies and needs my two best men? Next he'll be telling me that he needs me and Mims, too. Incompetent. He has a resident deputy in Halleck. Surely he could use him. How on earth did this man get elected?

Jack sat back on his heels, stirred the fire some more, and called Rob over. "I want you to hear what the sheriff just proposed, Rob, and then we'll need to have a long talk."

"I know I'm asking a lot, Jack, but there is a reason. Cattle are being rustled all over the county and I have men investigating the crimes. I have an open murder investigation at the Warren ranch, and now, it is probably a part of both those problems. The idea that cattle can be stolen and sold without consequence is something I've never considered. This would be the time a sheriff in Texas would call for the rangers. We don't have Nevada Rangers, Jack, but you do have a man who knows more about what the problem is than anyone else and I need him."

"What is it you're looking for, sheriff?" Rob poured a cup of coffee and sat down by the fire.

"You, Rob Slater. I want you to be my lead investigator on this. I want you to be an Elko County Deputy Sheriff and bring this operation down."

"No," Jack said. "Rob's not even eighteen yet, Sheriff. He can't wear a badge. I understand your position, but not your answer. What would Rob do that any other deputy couldn't do? The Slater family is well known in Halleck, so he sure couldn't go undercover."

"You got a better plan, Jack?" Sheriff Mossy Peacock was frustrated, fighting a rising anger, and still embarrassed by his lack of foresight with the Warren shootings.

"Not off the top of my head, Sheriff. No, I don't."

"I do," Rob said. Cactus Jack and Will Austin walked over and joined the group. "Glad you're here, Cactus. Will, I think you'll want to hear this too." Coffee was poured, sweetener was added and Rob continued.

"Duke Winston told us about the men who hung around Blake Wilson, who brought cattle to the feedlot. He understood them to be cattle buyers. We talked about this, Dad. They aren't cattle buyers, they're rustlers."

"You mean Belafleur, the Forbes brothers, and Odie Jackson. Those are the men who were always around Warren's but didn't work for Warren." Will Austin said, and Rob nodded.

"You need people to follow them out from Wilson's," Rob said. "Actually see them steal beef and sell it to Wilson. Somehow those cattle end up there with bills of sale. Find those blanks at Wilson's and it's all tied together."

"That's exactly what I wanted," Mossy Peacock said. "That's what I wanted Rob to do."

"Ain't no reason for me to do it, Sheriff when you have a man in Halleck." Rob smiled and poured a little more sweetener in his coffee. "Isn't that why you have resident deputies?"

Jack Slater found himself in a predicament tighter than any he had faced. His son, Rob, still so young but so far advanced for his age. Married, cow boss of the Slater operation, able, and probably willing to take on this incredibly dangerous mission. *He's my son, family. I can't ask him to risk his life like this.* And then Jack remembered his young life, leaving out from the Jablonski farm even younger than Rob is now.

He remembered Seth Bullock helping him grow into the man he is simply by being there. Remembered the ranch in Wyoming Territory and the rustlers he fought. Jack looked over at Rob, saw such a young face and such a large and strong body, saw a man, ready and eager to do the right thing. He saw himself and knew his answer.

"No badge, Mossy. No Rob unless I go, too." Jack saw Rob's face light up.

"You don't go, Jack, unless I go, too," Cactus Jack Faraday said. "We'll chase those banditos down in a week or less. I know that country, having worked for Ted Wilson for so long. Yeah, Sheriff, you got yourself a posse now. But I ain't carrying a badge."

"Oh, no, Cactus. You can't go. Who's gonna run my ranch," Jack said.

"Mr. Pettigrew, Two-dog Sorenson, and Will Austin," Cactus Jack said. "Let's not forget Tiny Howard, Tubs, and Pete Forrest."

Jack sat motionless for a moment or two, smiled at Rob, and said, "We'll leave out at daybreak. Don't you say anything about this, Mossy or I'll shoot you down. Nobody. Particularly your deputies." Mossy Peabody nodded with a smile and the group broke up.

"One other thing," Jack said. "You were there. You saw the action, took part in it. Why haven't you arrested Amos Warren for murder? He's moving around free as a bird, Sheriff and should be in irons."

"Puttin' together the whole investigation, Jack. It's coming, you can bet on that. With what I've learned and what I saw, Warren will be arrested soon."

Jack just shook his head, stood up and looked at his crew. "We'll travel light, boys. One pack horse, dried and smoked meat, coffee, flour, and sugar. Bring your long-glass Cactus and plenty of ammunition. We have a few names, we know what some of them look like, and that's all we have." He turned back to the sheriff.

"You better be prepared to back us up, Peabody."

Jack didn't sleep well that night, worrying if he was doing the right thing. *I've only had members of my family placed in danger when someone was threatening them. I'm the one placing Rob in danger. Am I doing the right thing? Is this really necessary? It's just stolen beef, and we're not the law.*

It wasn't just stolen beef and Jack knew that. It was Jake Winters' killing. It was the death of Ricardo Delgado. It was Wes Trimble's whole operation being threatened. It was the concept of a society living under the rule of law. "Maybe it really is family," he murmured.

He also had visions of Sonny Belafleur trying to attack him and Rob, of Amos Warren calling Rob a dirty Mex. He saw Rob gunning Belafleur down, saw himself beating the tar out of Warren, and knew these were the men stealing those beeves. He still wasn't fully satisfied that this was justified but also knew he was fully committed.

21

Wheeler and Odie Jackson were sitting at a table in a ranch house slightly north of Halleck. "This is better Jackson, me and Beer Belly are riding down to meet with Blake shortly. I want you to take Clint Sloan and show him around the countryside. We have to give the appearance of being able to work for Blake Wilson."

"We'll ride out through the valley north of here. Good pickin's out that way, even if we're not going to pick 'em," Jackson laughed. "We might need to pass through that area, though, after we hit Wilson."

"You can ride out anywhere you want, after. But you ain't ridin' out with us. You'll get your share just like we talked, but you ain't a part of this crew. Make sure Clint gets a good look at surrounding territory."

It was an hour's ride from the ranch house to the feedlot at Halleck and Wheeler and Beer Belly spent the time talking about how to take out Blake

Wilson, get the money out of the safe, and do away with Odie Jackson. "I'd just as soon shoot him as soon as that safe is opened up," Beer Belly said more than once.

"I'd sure like to know more about this Ling Ho character," Wheeler said. "You talked like you know the man. Is he as dangerous as you said, or were you just giving Jackson the razz."

"He's at least as dangerous as I said. His hands are his weapons, but he's good with knives, daggers, and swords too. I've never heard of him using a firearm, so if you stay back from him and shoot as soon as you see him, you might live." Beer Belly Bunker wasn't laughing.

"I'm wondering how best to get that safe opened," Wheeler said. "Killing Blake Wilson will be the easy part of this little plan, but getting him to open that safe before-hand won't be."

"He's a proud man, Henry," Beer Belly said. "Get him talking about how much money he's been making with this scam and he'll want to show it off. You might remember how he proudly showed that Pinkerton all the jewels he lifted from that New York woman. Got him five hard years at Huntsville."

They were still laughing as they dropped off a ridge and rode down to the feedlots. "Quite an operation he has," Wheeler said. "Pens aren't filled with fat cattle, though. That's why he needs us,

Beer Belly. That big building must be the offices. Spared no coin building it. Maybe Jackson really knows what he's talking about. Well, we know how to bring in the cows, don't we?"

"Henry Wheeler. Expected you yesterday. Come in, come in," Blake Wilson said. He had the door open before the men reached the top step and ushered them into the large great room. "Take the comfortable seats, boys," Wilson said. "Ling Ho, bring our guests some brandy, please."

"Make it whiskey," Wheeler snapped.

The tall, thin Chinese bowed ever so slightly and slipped out of the room as Wheeler and Beer Belly found overstuffed chairs to enjoy. "Hope you had a good trip, Henry. Where's Clint Sloan? You did bring him, didn't you?"

"Clint's with us, Henry. Let's go over this operation of yours. You have people for us as we asked?"

"Two very good men. I think you know Skinny Forbes and the other is Three-toes Jacobs. They've been with me from the start on this. Should be here shortly. This is a real money maker, Henry. I send the men out with blank bills of sale, they steal the cattle, fill in the blanks, alter the brands to match the bills of sale, and drive them here. Once they're accepted by the feedlot, ownership is never questioned. Since I own the feedlot, no questions are asked."

"It's a gold mine. I'm glad you want to be a part of it." Wilson sat back as Ling Ho came in with a decanter of brandy, a bottle of whiskey, and glasses. Try as he might, Henry Wheeler could not see a single weapon on the man. As the valet poured drinks Blake Wilson saw Skinny and Three-toes coming up the slope from the feedlot. "Looks like Skinny and Three-toes coming now. Better get a couple more glasses, Ling Ho."

Henry Wheeler continued watching the Chinese gentleman as he poured and handed out the drinks. He saw long, strong muscles in his arms, long fingers that could grasp a man's neck and hold it until death rattled about. The word formidable came to mind and he wondered if Ling Ho was also fast. *We don't want this man close by when we kill Blake and Odie. He could put the screws to our little plan quickly.*

"You've put on a pound or two, Skinny," Wheeler said when the men came in. "Looks like you're enjoying this prosperity Blake keeps talking about. Hello Three-toes."

"Still the glib tongue and a quick temper, eh Wheeler?" Skinny didn't offer his hand, instead took a drink of his brandy. "Got a couple of small ranches out in the north valley, all picked out for us. Figure we'll hit them late tonight and bring the cattle in late tomorrow. Okay with you, Blake?"

He was talking to Wilson, not Wheeler, and Wheeler didn't like that. "I'll want to see these steers and locations before we make any moves, Skinny. Blake brought me and the boys in because you haven't been doing a very good job of providing beef. You're working for me now, and we do things my way."

"Ain't the way it is, Henry." It had been a long time since anyone talked to Skinny that way and he wasn't going to take it. *You'd best be careful how you talk, Henry. We've done a fine job and will keep doing a fine job.* "We work for Blake, Henry, but will work with you. You will need to work with us, too." Skinny Forbes wasn't going to wait to establish the rules of the game and stood next to a heavy oak table, his right hand casually close to the big gun at his waist.

Blake Wilson watched as the game continued to play out. He saw Beer Belly Bunker move slightly away from Wheeler and saw Three-toes match the move. He also saw Ling Ho move so as to protect Blake if gunfire erupted. Blake needed to make his move first.

"Skinny's right, Henry. They work for me and we'll all work together on this operation. For it to succeed, I need to fill those pens out there. The five of you can do that and we all make a lot of money. Let's have an early supper here tonight and you can all ride out to gather some steers."

Tensions eased, slowly and the men all drank their brandies and whiskies, letting conversation turn to making brands on the go. Henry Wheeler was an expert and he talked about just having short pieces of iron, some straight, some slightly curved, some strongly curved. "With those, you can turn almost any brand into something else, and you don't need to carry fifty pounds of iron with you."

"Well, more of this at supper," Blake said. "Ling Ho will have supper on the table at six, gentlemen. I'll see you then." The meeting was over and Wilson knew he was going to be faced with problems over and over, because of the way Wheeler and Forbes felt about each other.

"There are five men visiting with Blake Wilson right now, Jack, and they aren't dressed for supper, either." Cactus Jack said. He and Rob had been watching the feedlot most of the day from a grove of trees just below the ridge line. "I didn't recognize anyone of them."

"Same ones as earlier today. The only one I recognized was Skinny Forbes. Maybe we should have brought Will Austin with us," Cactus Jack said.

"We'd best be ready to follow if they're planning on rustling some cattle tonight," Jack Slater said. "The cattle have almost all been rustled late at night, so they might ride out soon."

They moved with their horses from the rough camp down the ridge and into a grove of cotton-wood trees where they could keep close watch on the office building. The sun was just setting when Henry Wheeler led the five to their horses. Jack Slater could see Blake Wilson standing on the porch, watching them ride off.

"Let's go, boys, but quietly and not too close."

It was a quick ten mile ride to a ranch sitting west of Mary's River and they watched from a few hundred yards out as the five men cut a fence, moved twelve steers quietly off their pasture, and five miles into a small closed canyon.

"That was so quick and quiet I wouldn't have believed it if I hadn't seen it," Cactus Jack said. They tied their horses off and moved closer to where Skinny Forbes had a good fire burning. Jack and the crew were hunkered down in rocks and brush watching the operation. "They've done this more than once. Nobody's missing a beat," Cactus said.

It was like watching a clock work, Rob thought. One at a time, Three-toes or Beer Belly would heel a steer and drag it to the fire where Wheeler would alter the brand to match what would be on the bill of sale. Sloan and Skinny would then move the steer to a brush holding pen.

Sunrise came early late in the spring and the outlaws had the small herd moving well before first light. They kept an easy pace through open range, arriving at the feedlot in the early afternoon. Blake Wilson came out to welcome them. "Good job, boys. Get some sleep. Henry, bring all the paperwork up to the office."

Blake Wilson could almost see the money rolling in. Twelve to fifteen cows every other day or so and he'd have that packing house humming again. More than that, he'd be putting wads of cash in his safe. *My only problem is going to be keeping Wheeler from killing Forbes or the other way around.* He almost snickered, thinking about it.

"What I wanted to talk to you about, Henry is how you and the boys want to be paid. I've always paid these men once a month, in cash, of course, after a fine meal up here at the office."

"Me and the boys like our money right away. We've already had this conversation, Blake, so don't be trying to change things." Blake could see the anger building in the man. "I won't allow changes, Wilson. Won't!"

"No changes, Henry, just details. You just brought twelve head in. Do you want to be paid right now, or wait until you've brought, say fifty head in? It's entirely up to you."

Wheeler settled down, stood by Blake's desk and thought about it. If he took the money now, it would be him alone with Blake. Easy to kill him after he opened the safe to get the money. But, would it be easy? There was always Ling Ho close by. It would be better to have all the boys there, at supper and a big show by Wilson getting all that money from the safe. And all those guns keeping Ling Ho at bay.

"I like the idea of having a nice supper with the added attraction of a lot of money being distributed, Blake. Let's say, uh, after our next delivery. That must be quite a safe you have. I think I heard Three-toes mention it."

"It's a wonderful safe, Henry. Big," he said, opening his arms wide. "Too big for someone to want to try and haul it off." He laughed, but it almost sounded like a challenge to Henry Wheeler. "Intricate, too. Have to be precise opening it. Had it made special in Philadelphia and shipped out."

Wheeler remembered Big Belly's comments about Blake Wilson being a proud man and tested the thought. "I'd like to see that," Henry Wheeler said.

Blake smiled and motioned Wheeler to follow and they walked to what looked like a set of curtains in front of a window. "You'll love this," he said. When the curtains were drawn, there was a wall safe, not a window.

"Well, will you look at that. A fake wall, Blake?" Wheeler was impressed, got right up to the safe, tapped on the surrounding wall, and looked left and right to see. "Fake wall," he said again.

"Only partially fake, Henry. Just look at that thing. Need six horses up to haul that off, eh?"

"Must hold a ton, Blake." Wheeler was trying to figure out just how big the safe was and decided that he better stop Blake from showing more. A man this willing to talk about what he has will be easy, but Henry knew he had to wait for the right time. For when he had all his guns with him.

As he turned from the safe, there was Ling Ho, less than five feet behind him and he never knew the man was there. *He came up behind me as quiet as dust settling on a table. Could have slit my throat in an instant.*

22

"I sent a wire to Mossy Peabody," Jack Slater said. They were settled around a small fire at the little rough camp. "He'll be here sometime tomorrow. Anything going on down below?" From their position along the ridge, they could look down on the entire Wilson project.

"That one big fellow, the one who seems to be directing everything rode off and I followed," Rob said. "He went to a ranch near Mary's River and met with Odie Jackson. That was a surprise, Dad. Why would he do that?"

Jack Slater sat back on his heels, poured a cup of coffee and let a slow smile come across his face. "I would say that Blake Wilson might be in for a big surprise sometime soon." Odie Jackson was part of the Belafleur/Warren set up and Jack saw that Wilson would face a problem right away.

"Me, too," Cactus Jack said. "There's some kind

of double cross in someone's plans, Jack. Odie Jackson and Skinny Forbes both worked for Sonny Belafleur. But I don't know any of these other fellers."

"We'll stay as tight to them as we can, then and hope to catch them in the act, whatever that might be. What kind of double-cross are you thinking of, Cactus?" Jack was seeing a takeover, but couldn't put a real handle on it.

"You might remember telling me about your conversation with that Duke Winston feller. He said Wilson always had considerable cash on hand. With Belafleur dead, the gang busted up, Odie might have brought some people in to rip Mr. Wilson off."

"You might be right. Think they'll ride out again tonight?" Jack Slater wanted to put the lid on this and get back to his ranch. They had been away for too many days.

"They're packing up right now, Dad." Rob pointed at the five men, saddle bags filled, getting ready to ride out. "They're pretty clever the way they take the fences down. Makes it look like some angry heifer broke out and the rest followed."

"And the rancher is busy rounding up his strays and doesn't know he's been robbed until the count begins." Cactus Jack Faraday had a grim look on his face. "Old Mr. Trimble was lucky."

"We're heading further west tonight, boys, into those rocky ridges and spiny pines. Should be able to pick up fifteen head or more from old Bellow's place. Run 'em into the same canyon we used the other night." Skinny Forbes had ridden this range several times recently and knew where the best cattle were.

"Need some place closer, Skinny," Wheeler said. "Some place with more animals, too. Maybe bring in twenty five or more tonight."

"We just went through all that with Sonny Belafleur, Henry. That's what destroyed what we had going. Take small groups often is Blake's plan and we're stickin' to it."

"He brought us in because you couldn't fill his pens with cows, Skinny. Plans change," Wheeler said. "We're going for twenty five or more. I'd just as soon it be fifty head. What do you say, Beer Belly?"

"We can fix fifty before sunup, Henry, if the brand's an easy one to fix. No more than that. Yeah, fifty'll work."

"You're gonna end up the same as Belafleur, Wheeler. And he's dead."

"You ain't got it in you to go up against me and my boys, Forbes. We're going for fifty head, whether you're in or not. I'm runnin' this show, now."

They were a mile or two from Charlie Bellows' holding pasture. He would be moving his herd into the high country in the next few days, according to what Skinny Forbes knew. "You take that many head and sure as the sun's gonna shine in the morning, Charlie Bellows will follow with his hands. We cut the fences right, take fifteen or so and let the rest wander about, and we'll be free. You ain't thinking, Wheeler, just like always."

"You're talkin' hog wallow. We're takin' everything that old man has." Wheeler turned in the saddle, his sidearm in hand, and fired point blank into Skinny Forbes' mid-section, knocking the man to the ground.

Forbes rolled around in the rocks and dirt, blood flowing freely. He had enough strength left to pull his revolver and fire off a shot, blowing a gash in the side of Wheeler's horse, causing the horse to throw a bucking fit. Wheeler fell to the ground and Clint Sloan made a quick ride to catch the wounded horse. Forbes pulled himself up on one elbow and fired again, striking Wheeler high in his right leg.

Wheeler spun around, his gun blazing, and put two shots into Forbes, killing him. "Get my horse," Wheeler yelled.

"Dead, Henry," Clint said. "Bullet ripped him open. You'll have to take Skinny's nag. I'll change the saddles, make sure you've got your workin' iron. Better get that leg fixed up before you join your horse."

Wheeler spun on Three-toes Jacobs. "You with us or you gonna join Forbes? Your choice right now and I don't care what it is. Two dead ain't no different than one dead to me."

"I don't think you're right, but I'm here for the money, Wheeler. Always have been, I guess. Better bury him, though. A stinkin' body is sure to draw attention."

Wheeler snickered, turned to Beer Belly and Sloan. "Take the time, or not."

"Time's already short, Henry," Beer Belly Bunker said. "Cows are waitin', but your leg ain't. Need to get that fixed up." Beer Belly looked at Three-toes, then at Forbes' body. "Drag him off the trail and throw some rocks on him while I patch up Henry."

There was the slightest hesitation and Beer Belly Bunker thought sure as all get-out there would be another body to dispose of, but Three-toes stepped down from his saddle and started dragging Forbes off into the desert.

"Come here, Henry. Can you ride when I get you patched? We're running out of time. Gonna be sunrise before we move a single cow."

"I'm about ready to call it off, Beer Belly. We've made enough noise to raise the dead." He was trying to talk through serious pain as Bunker worked to get his pants cut away and get the blood flow stopped. "Gonna have a stinkin' body right where we have to bring the cows through, too." He looked toward the eastern horizon and saw that it was starting to lighten up some. "Can't break them cows out when it's light, boys and we can't get there before it's light."

"Wilson ain't gonna like this, Henry," Clint Sloan said.

"He ain't gonna like it when we empty his safe tonight, either." Henry Wheeler hurt like all get-out but still laughed right out. "Yeah, boys, we take him out tonight." He looked Clint in the eye. "Why don't you ride on out to Odie's and tell him to be there about six for the party."

Clint Sloan rode out to the combined laughter from Beer Belly Bunker and Henry Wheeler. Three-toes Jacobs was making plans of his own as he moved some rocks on top of Skinny Forbes' body.

"He gunned Skinny down in cold blood, Jack. I was just a hundred yards away. I could hear almost every word said. They were talking about moving toward Charlie Bellows' place, but called it off. We could get that big feller for murder right now."

"We could, Cactus, but that wouldn't stop the packing house operation. Let's stick with our plan. You were a witness to murder, Cactus and we witnessed the rustling the other night. Tonight we'll miss this one, I guess. We're two-thirds of the way to stopping this whole criminal operation and the sheriff and his people will be here later today. Let's let it play out."

"I was close enough to hear the big feller send that other one off to get Odie Jackson. Something's gonna happen tonight, Jack."

"That name just continues to pop up. He rode for Sonny Belafleur and was attached to Warren. Some of these other fellers are newcomers, I think." Rob Slater was shaking his head. "I hope we get a chance to talk with this Blake Wilson. I have a million questions for the man."

"Let's head back to our little camp, boys and see what we can figure out. We need to keep close watch on these men. Willing to kill in cold blood and take what isn't theirs, we're dealing with the meanest of outlaws."

Jack knew there was a lot more at play than rustling a few head of cattle. More even than selling stolen cattle through the feedlot. *What is it that's going to happen? We've got enough to hang that one man, but not stop Wilson. Almost enough. Those men coming back to the feedlot will have the proof of sale papers with them, but the brand mark will be blank. Or will it? They were riding toward Bellows, maybe they had a change-up from Bellows' brand already on the sales-slip. We'll just have to let this one play out. Glad Mossy and his boys will be here.*

23

Wilson was in a rage when Wheeler, Beer Belly, and Three-toes rode into the feedlot empty handed. "Not one beef and you killed one of my men? Why'd you even come back? Might as well have kept riding, Wheeler, cuz you ain't working for me. Pack it up and move it out."

"Hold your temper, Wilson. We'll get fifty head for you tomorrow. Your man pulled down on me and got what he deserved," Henry Wheeler lied. "We wanted fifty head and he was afraid to take that many, that's all. Got himself all in an uproar about us taking fifty head." He limped a step or two toward Wilson, but the feedlot operator stood his ground.

"The plan has always been ten to fifteen head two or three times a week, Henry. You know that as well as the man you killed. You got greedy, just like Sonny Belafleur and you're gonna pay for that."

"You ain't talkin' to me that way, Blake Wilson." Henry Wheeler's anger took over and he made a fast grab for his revolver, only to find himself flung backwards and in terrible pain, his right arm, almost severed and bleeding heavily. Ling Ho stood over him, a wicked smile on his face, a bloody and menacing sword in his hands. Ling Ho raised the sword with both hands and was about to swing it toward Wheeler, as if to decapitate the man.

"No," Wheeler cried out. Blake Wilson clapped his hands once and Ling Ho held up and eased the sword back down. Beer Belly Bunker started to step forward and Ling Ho had the sword up and ready to slash. Bunker stopped immediately.

"Smart, Beer Belly," Wilson snickered. "Better take care of your man. Gonna bleed out soon if you don't. Three-toes, follow me to the office. Ling Ho, escort these men off the property as soon as Wheeler's tended to." Wilson turned and headed for the office building with Three-toes right behind him.

"I need to know exactly what happened out there, Three-toes. Then, we need to have a long talk."

This is my chance, what I've been waiting for. Three-toes had a hint of smile as he followed Wilson up the long path to the office. *I'll be alone with him and Ling Ho will not be there to protect him. Only need to get him to get that safe open.*

Jack Slater, Rob, and Cactus were sitting in the rocks on the ridge above the feedlot, watching all the going's on below. "I've never seen anything like that in my life," Rob Slater said. "My God, he almost cut his arm right off."

"It was his head that was next," Cactus Jack said. "That's some kind of short broad sword that boy's carrying. Sheriff and his men should be arriving any minute, Jack. You think we ought to move on them fellows before somebody dies?"

"No, it'll be Mossy's play when they get here, Cactus. Those men were planning something for tonight but I have to believe that's been changed. Sure wish we could follow Three-toes and Wilson into the office. I think Wilson's operation is coming apart as we watch, but it's the packing house/feedlot combination that needs to be shut down."

"This operation needs to halted. You're right about that, Dad." Rob Slater was thinking about next week and the future, not what was happening as they watched. "The cattlemen need to demand new laws on branding, moving, and selling cattle. If nothing else comes of this, those new laws must come about or sure as all get out we'll see more Blake Wilsons come forward."

"Ted Wilson would be proud of you right now, Son." Jack Slater stopped to listen to something and Cactus Jack jumped to his feet and was running back toward their camp. "Let's go," Jack said. He and Rob were right behind Cactus and pulled up short seeing Mossy Peabody step down from his horse.

"You just missed a fine show, Sheriff," Cactus Jack said. "Mighty fine show, indeed."

Jack Slater stepped forward quickly. "Your men riding up behind you, Sheriff?"

"I didn't bring anyone with me, Jack. Didn't think I'd need to, with you three here."

"Hope you're right," Slater mumbled. *The man just got a new name as far as I'm concerned. From now on it's Sheriff No Backup. He really is a fool and a show-boat on top of it. I don't have good feelings right now.*

"You just assumed that the four of us would be enough to take out Wilson and his gang? Sheriff, you gotta get your head on straight. These men are known killers." Slater stomped around for a minute or so and finally just plopped down next to the fire. "All right, then. Here's what we're looking at."

The group sat around the fire, had coffee cups full, and Jack Slater outlined what had happened so far. They were interrupted by gunfire coming from down below. "Looks like your party is still going on, Jack. Let's ride down there," Peabody said.

"Things are changing and not for the good, Three-toes. Once again, my friend, it's just the two of us and unless I get some cattle in those pens out there, this operation will come to a fast halt. Those contracts are coming due fast. I have a couple of ideas and you're a big part of those plans. Did Skinny Forbes really draw on Wheeler?"

"He argued hard, but, no. Wheeler simply shot him down like a dirty dog. You better have some good plans, Blake, or I'm riding out. All that's happening is sure to bring the law down on us and I mean soon."

"That's why I need you. I'm gonna give you some hard cash, Three-toes." Blake Wilson was talking as he walked toward the curtains hiding the big safe. "I want you to ride to Elko, Winnemucca, Battle Mountain, maybe even Austin and buy us some good hands. Maybe three, but four or five would be better. If you bring me good hands in the next week or so, we can save this operation."

I'm not even going to have to con him into opening that safe. He's gonna open it and I'm gonna shoot him dead. Three-toes' mind was spinning as he tried to figure out how to get away after shooting Wilson and stuffing as much of that money in to something as he could carry. What would he use to haul it out? One gunshot and Mr. Chinese killer would be in the room with that ugly sword.

Three-toes saw that Wilson wasn't paying him any attention and eased to the front door, twisting the key in the lock and slipping it in his pocket.

I can't run that way for sure but neither can that assassin get in.

Wilson walked up to the curtains and drew them back, turned the dial several times, and Three-toes didn't move a muscle until that massive door swung open. Two big 45-70 bullets slammed into Blake Wilson, both coming out the other side. Three-toes jumped forward, pushed the body out of the way, and grabbed hands-full of banded U.S. currency. "That man had a way about him. Even bound his bills into packages. Thanks for that, Blake."

He was laughing loud as he stuffed packet after packet inside his shirt, until there wasn't any more room. He looked about, couldn't see anything he could stuff more money into, and ran for the kitchen and the back door.

"What was that?" Beer Belly Bunker was kneeling next to Henry Wheeler, trying to get his arm put back together and not having much luck. "Two shots, Henry, came from the office."

"Three-toes," Beer Belly muttered and started to run toward the office. Ling Ho knocked him down with a solid chop to the neck and raced for the big building. He was a gifted runner and leaped to the porch, ignoring the steps. He slammed into the heavy doors of the office, thinking they would be flung open, and bounced back.

Ling Ho raced down the porch toward a set of windows and broke the glass with his sword, stepping into the great room. Blake Wilson was sprawled in a pool of blood near the open safe and Ling Ho raced for the kitchen and the back door, saw Three-toes throwing a saddle on a horse near the corral. The Chinese gentleman never carried a firearm, always depended on his knives, batons, and swords, and he vaulted from the back porch for the race across the wide yard.

Three-toes was in the saddle well before the assassin reached the area and raced off, just using the lead rope and halter in place of bridle and reins. He was an excellent horseman and was into the mountainous country to the north. He turned down off the slopes into the valley to the east and put that horse in a full wide-open gallop.

"If I can make Wells, I can get on a train and be gone from this country forever." He talked loud to the horse, to himself, and to the winds as he raced across the broad, brush and pine covered high mountain desert. It would be a long ride and after about fifteen minutes of hard riding, Three-toes eased the horse down to a walk. *Won't use you up in one hard run, big boy. Gonna need all that speed again, I'm sure. Sure glad old Blake always kept the best horses.*

Sheriff Peabody led Jack Slater, Rob, and Cactus down off the ridge and into the feedlot. Beer Belly was still working on Henry Wheeler. "Got yourself pretty well mangled there," Peabody said. "What's the shootin' all about?"

"Who are you?" Beer Belly asked.

"I'm the sheriff, and you two are under arrest. Pull that gun and ease it to the ground." Peabody waved his pistol to move Beer Belly back and picked up the weapon. He reached down and relieved Wheeler of his, too. "Again, What's the shootin' all about."

"Don't know. It was up at the house," Wheeler said. He was barely conscious, but pointed toward the office building.

Slater and company were already making their way up the pathway toward the porch when Ling Ho unlocked and opened the front doors. Slater had his weapon in hand and stopped as soon as the Chinese appeared. "Don't move," he said. Ling Ho was looking at three big guns aimed at him and stopped.

"Boss man shot dead. Money stole," the assassin said, nodding toward the open doors. "Man run north on horse. Must hurry."

He stepped aside and Slater led everyone inside the great room. Along with Blake Wilsons perforated body they found a few bundles of cash spread in front of the massive vault. "That's a lot of cash," Cactus Jack said. "There's still more inside the safe. No wonder everyone was so willing to kill. I'll get Peabody."

Slater allowed Ling Ho to show him through the kitchen and pointed out where Three-toes found the getaway horse. "He ride that way," Ling Ho said. Jack turned to go back through the house to get everyone on the trail.

"Now you know why you needed to bring men with you, Sheriff." Jack said. "We've got to get on that man's trail. He left out north but you can bet lots of money that he turned east. He needs to get a lot of miles between us and fast."

"I really didn't think we'd need any," Peabody said.

"No back up?" Cactus Jack howled at the man. "You came out from Elko to bring this gang down all by yourself? Now what are you going to do? You've got a dead man in there, a trained assassin with swords and knives, and two prisoners, one seriously injured. How did you ever get to be sheriff with that kind of thinking."

"Easy, Cactus," Jack Slater said. He turned and gave Peabody a withering look. "You didn't learn anything at the Warren ranch? I ought to just gather my boys and ride on home, Mossy, but I'm not that kind of man. For your information, there's a man out there somewhere on a stolen horse packing several thousands in stolen money that he took after killing the owner of the horse and money." Jack was yelling at Peabody almost as loud as Cactus Jack had been. He tried to hold his anger in, but it was this kind of stupidity that fired off Jack Slater.

"Whoever's going to chase that man should get started soon," Rob said with a snicker. "And somebody needs to get into Halleck and send a wire for backup." He kicked some dirt around. "You might be right, Dad."

"The killer has to be caught, but we're here to shut this place down. Search these two men and see if they might have drawings of what old man Bellows' brand might be altered to, and see if there are bills of sale in some other name. We can at least end this operation."

"Sheriff, put these men in cuffs and ride into Halleck. Send out some wires to look for Three-toes, form up a posse, and bring help for this wounded one. Rob, you and Cactus ride up and break camp and be quick about it."

Peabody cuffed Beer Belly to Wheeler and walked toward his horse for the short ride into town while Rob and Cactus jumped on their rides and headed up the slope to gather their camp. Jack smiled when he found the paperwork he was look-ing for in Wheelers' coat pocket. "Well, this seals it."

"Watch out," Beer Belly screamed and Jack rolled hard off to his left, pulling his sidearm as he did. The razor sharp blade of a short broad sword whistled past his ear and buried itself in the dirt next to him. The big Colt belched fire twice and flung Ling Ho back ten feet. The Chinese's body jerked a couple of times and became still.

"Appreciate that, Mr. Bunker. I won't forget it." Jack Slater eased up to the dead assassin, kicked him to make sure he was dead, and eased the sword from his hands. Slater stood still for a moment wondering why the man would attack him. They were alone inside, the Chinese gentleman pointed out where Three-toes ran off, and now, tries to kill him.

I think this means I'm going to find a lot of evidence inside that office. It also means we need a lot more people than we have. What are we going to do about Peabody? He just isn't made to be a sheriff. He should have had at least three or four men with him.

Slater moved the two prisoners out of the sun and into shade from a cottonwood tree, moved Ling Ho's body too, and walked up the steps to the feedlot office. *I just hope that Wilson was the kind of man who kept records. Shouldn't have to be doing this. Peabody should be doing it. All this time has gone by and Three-toes is riding toward freedom.*

Rob and Cactus were back at the feedlot in quick time and found Jack in the office holding a sheaf of papers. "This Blake Wilson kept detailed records, Rob. You're gonna have the time of your life interpreting all of this. He even has drawings of how best to make new brands out of many of the existing brands in the county."

Slater smiled and walked to a large overstuffed chair and sat down. "Time for a chat, boys. We have dead that need to taken care of, prisoners that need to be taken care of, and an escaped murderer who needs to be caught. What we don't seem to have is a sheriff who can think. Who wants to go first?"

24

"Do we join the chase for Three-toes or just ride on home and let Peabody stew in his own stupidity?" Rob was leafing through page after page of material that would have sent Blake Wilson to prison had he lived. "These papers along with everything we witnessed will end this operation. Blake Wilson's scheme is over and the only thing left is catching a murdering horse thief."

"Mossy isn't up to leading a posse on a chase like what I'm thinkin' it will be." Cactus Jack settled in a chair across from Jack. "I never have been much for leavin' a job only half done."

"Those are pretty much my thoughts," Rob said. "I'd like to see to it that the sheriff has all these papers and understands their importance, though. He might just ride off and leave them sitting around or something. Catching the murderer is important, but these papers will allow the cattlemen to work on new laws preventing this from happening again. He has to be made to understand that."

"You've got mighty quiet, Cactus," Slater said. "Give it out, old man. What are you thinking?"

"Rob should be sheriff," Cactus said. He sat with a little boy's grin, shaking his head, got up and walked over to the still open safe. "A lot of other people's cattle represented here. Can't leave this half finished, Jack just because the sheriff ain't too bright."

"I agree. Rob?"

"Me, too, Dad."

"Where would you run to, Cactus. I'd want to find a train and it wouldn't matter whether it was going east or west." Slater said

"Three-toes knows this country well, Jack." Cactus Jack was still pacing around the room. "He'll be in Wells tomorrow if he rides hard and once he's on a train, he's gone."

"It's late in the day, Dad. Even if we took the main road, he's got a big jump on us." Rob sat dejected, thinking they would lose their man. They had two live prisoners, all the paperwork in the world to shut the operation down, but the one getting away was a murdering horse thief who needed to be caught. "He'll catch that train east in the morning and be gone."

"What if we're on that train, Rob?" Slater sat back with a big smile on his face.

"Son of a gun," Cactus yelled out. "No wonder I work for you. We better get into town."

Cactus was finishing tying Beer Belly Bunker and Henry Wheeler to their horses as Mossy Peabody and two men rode in to the feedlot. "Two men? That's it?" Slater was about to just storm off, but kept his temper in check.

"Listen close, Sheriff. There's a stack of papers on the desk that need to go directly to the district attorney. Every single sheet. That's a priority. Take care of this mess here. We'll catch Three-toes." He walked to where Rob and Cactus were standing with their horses. "Mount up, boys, we've got work to do."

Peabody just stood in the sunlight, never said a word, and watched Slater and the boys ride off. "Let's bury the dead," he finally said.

The ride into town was a short one and they tied off at the train station, bought tickets, and arranged for the horses, too. "Train'll be here in a couple of hours and we'll be in Wells in the morning. I don't know about you two, but I haven't eaten anything since those cold biscuits at sunrise." They were smiling as they took seats in a restaurant across from the depot.

Three-toes kept that fine horse of Blake Wilson's at a ground eating trot most of the way to Wells, slowing only to let the big animal catch its breath. The day was hot but when night came, it seemed to have winter written broadly in its winds. Three-toes wasn't prepared for a cold night and there was no slicker or even bedroll tied off behind the saddle he grabbed.

The cold wind blew down on him from the north east as he rode east from Halleck and by the time he saw lights from Wells, he was frozen to the bone. Would they be looking for him? He wondered about that and how he could protect all that cash money he was carrying. He rode off the main street and circled around, coming up from the south on the still closed depot. "Gotta get warm," he muttered tying off. There was a café and saloon across the street and he knew he was taking a big chance, but walked into the saloon.

It was late, only a few men left inside, some at the bar, some at the gaming tables. His almost desperate search didn't produce a single badge, though. There was a large pot-belly stove in the center of the room and Three-toes stood close to it for a couple of minutes. Three-toes had his hat down low, the collar of his light jacket pulled up as he moved to the bar and ordered whiskey from the barman. "Cold," he said.

"Happens every year," the barman said. "This is the late spring storm that seems to come every year. Drink hearty, my friend and you'll soon be warm."

The jovial man, skinny as a rail but wearing a massive full beard, started to walk on down the bar.

"Question," Three-toes said, and the man turned back. "What time does the ticket office at the train station open?"

"Morning east-bound special will be here at six, so they will be open by five, I'm sure. Where you heading for?"

"Chicago," Three-toes said. It was the first thing that popped into his mind. "Never been there, but I got a brother works for the Swift Company." He knew he was babbling and had to stop, took the time to slowly pour out a drink and sipped some. "That'll warm me up. Thanks."

He waited until the barman turned to walk away before he tried to extract a bill from one of the packets. He almost ripped it and found he had to tear the binding before he could a get one loose. *Gotta get one loose. Come on, rip.* He looked around quickly to make sure no one was looking, got a bill free, and laid it out on the bar.

He looked out the dirty windows of the saloon and saw the dawn slowly breaking forth, figured it was probably coming five, and finished his whiskey. He motioned for the barman, paid him, waited impatiently for his change, and made his way out. He watched a deputy walk down the street and go into the train station, turned, and walked the other way down the street.

"Can't get caught," he muttered. "Not now. Not with all this money. I'm rich, for the first time in my life, I'm rich. I ain't losing it." He stood in the shadows of two buildings and watched the deputy walk out of the station and go across the street to the café. "Did he tell the ticket master to watch for me? Why did he go in there?"

Three-toes circled around behind the station and came in from the south, track side entrance. He stopped to make sure his horse was still there and ventured into the building. He sidled up to another pot-belly stove, now almost red hot. He could only see the ticket master and rather boldly walked to the window. "One for Denver, please, sir. Sleeping car, if you don't mind."

"Baggage?" The ticket master never even looked up.

"Just what I'm carrying. Is there a layover in Salt Lake?"

"No, this is straight through to Denver. They switch in Denver. That'll be twelve dollars, please. Train'll arrive at six and depart at six-ten sharp. Have a good trip."

It took minutes for Three-toes to relax as he stepped out onto the platform to wait for the train. The whiskey in his belly was warm and he still felt the effects of the stove. "Must have just been one of his morning stops," Three-toes said. "Deputy wasn't putting out the word to watch for me."

He wasn't aware, but when Sheriff Peabody rode into Halleck to find a posse and put out the word to watch for Three-toes, he sent the wire to his Elko office for them to follow through. No wires had been sent to the resident deputies individually. If Peabody had made a simple stop at the resident deputy's office, and the word had been sent out, Three-toes would already be in jail. Three-toes carefully took a look around the corner of the station at the café across the street and saw the deputy sitting at the counter.

"Sure could use some of that coffee and a pork chop or two to go with it. Cold," he murmured. The large clock inside said five-forty-five and the outlaw walked briskly back and forth on the platform, constantly looking down the long steel rails for the train. People were coming into the station house, buying tickets, bringing luggage out to the platform, some complaining about the cold.

"He said six. Where's that train?"

"Gettin' light, Jack. Should be coming up on Wells shortly," Cactus Jack said. He nudged the big rancher and jostled Rob on the bench next to him. "Rise and shine, boys, we got a day full of chasing murderers."

"It ain't natural for a man to be that happy this early in the morning." Rob rubbed his eyes, stood up and tried to stretch, but was too tall for the coach. "All right, I'm up, Cactus. Let the day begin."

"All right, boys," Slater said. "Been thinking how to do this. As soon as the train stops, Cactus, I want you out on that platform looking for Three-toes. Rob, you need to make your way as fast as you can to get the horses out, just in case Three-toes sees us and makes a break for it. I'll stay on board and watch for your signal, Cactus."

Jack looked to make sure both nodded back to him. "You'll have to keep a close eye on Cactus, too, Rob. Whatever car Three-toes gets on, you follow him, Cactus and we'll join you. He's not quick with his guns, but he is with his knives, so watch for him to grab someone as a hostage when we approach."

They could feel the coach begin to slow and Cactus and Rob moved toward the coach platform. "Think he'll run?" Rob asked.

"Shore as I'm Texas," Cactus laughed.

25

Andy Pettigrew walked over to the small fire Two-dog Sorenson had going near the south entrance to the barn. "Cold this morning, Two-dog. Supposed to be spring. Seen anything?" Light was spreading across the vast Nevada sky and Pettigrew was about to relieve Two-dog on barn watch.

"Thought I heard horses once, Andy, but never was able to see anything. I sent Tiny Howard out to check, but he couldn't find anything out of line. Jack was sure that Amos Warren would try something while he was gone. Man can't really be that stupid."

"Better talk to Will Austin, Two-dog." Pettigrew laughed. "Who's riding fence this morning?"

"Pete Forrest is on north fence with Tubs, and Tiny rode out with Will Austin to move those calves south of us. Seems too early for pasture rotation, but we haven't had any rain for some time this spring. Barn's all yours, Andy. I'm gonna catch a nap and ride out to help with the calves. Yell loud if you need something."

Two-dog walked to the kitchen to grab a sweet roll and coffee before hitting the sack. "Morning, Mims, howdy Wanda. It was a long quiet night out there. Need some of your tender loving coffee and sweet rolls."

"Coming right up, Mr. Two-dog," Wanda said, curtsying and laughing. "Are you always bright and cheerful this early in the morning?"

"Only if I think there might be coffee and sweet rolls available," he joked. "Any of the others checked in?" He sat down at the table and used his fork to grab a sweet roll, still warm, and dripping with glazed sugar. "Didn't see Houlihan once during the night."

"He hasn't come in, Two-dog." Mims said. "The day crew left out half an hour ago."

"He is supposed to be protecting the house and bunk house. I better go out and check." Two-dog Sorenson walked quickly to the barn to saddle his horse. "Something ain't right," he muttered. He rode out the south entrance of the barn.

"Andy, Jimmy Houlihan hasn't checked in. I'm gonna ride the circuit. Keep your ears open." He rode out and around the barn pens, circled the breaking corrals, remuda pens, and was about to make the wide turn east to get around the bunkhouse and hog pens when he spotted a saddled horse standing near a cottonwood tree.

It was Houlihan's pinto and it stood quietly, chomping on fresh grass when Two-dog rode up. He stepped down and took up the Pinto's reins, dragging in the grass. The first thing Two-dog saw was cold blood on the saddle. "No, no," he muttered. He trailed the pinto quickly back to the barn and yelled for Pettigrew before he tied it off.

"We got us a problem, Andy. Looks like Jimmy's hurt." He pointed at the blood spots on the saddle. "Found the horse down by the cottonwood. We could sure use another person right now. Ride out and find Will Austin while I start the search for Houlihan. Keep that rifle of yours at the ready."

"That goes for you, too, old friend." Andy Pettigrew was saddled and Two-dog watched him ride off at a fast lope in minutes. Sorenson rode back to where he found the pinto and started looking for sign. He found where the pinto came into the little glade and slowly back tracked. The wind was picking up, from the north and it had a winter's bite to it.

He rode through a tangle of pine, cottonwood, and scrub brush along a gully that was often filled with rabbits, quail, and mule deer. Water ran through it during spring and early summer and Sorenson noted the pinto had stopped to graze along the top of the ditch.

Two-dog stepped down from his horse to untie the heavy coat he had strapped under his rain poncho and could feel the wind from the bullet that passed his ear. The shot came from the gully off to his left and he hit the ground, rolling, snaked his way to a pine tree, and had his Colt in hand.

"Better give it up, Mister. I got friends comin' fast and I'm one of the meanest on this range." Two-Dog reached down to make sure he had his knife handy and remembered he was carrying one made by Jennifer Trimble. "Good," he muttered.

He heard rustling noises from the gully and it sounded like someone mounting a horse. "That's the noise I heard last night." He half crawled, half ran to the gully's edge and saw a man trying to get on a spooked horse.

"Hold it up or die," Two-dog yelled. He jumped down into the tangled brush, the Colt aimed at the man's mid-section. "Gonna get my man early," he said. "Drop the reins and get flat on the ground. Ain't gonna say it again."

The man whirled and put a shot into Sorenson's leg, knocking him to the ground. Two-dog fired one back, hitting the man in the arm, just below his elbow, knocking the gun loose. The man grabbed it up with his left hand and fired again, missing Two-dog, but knocking Sorenson's gun right out of his hand. Two-dog reached for his knife with his good hand and started to crawl toward the gunman.

Two shots rang out and the intruder died when hot lead blew through his heart. "You good, Two-dog?" Andy Pettigrew climbed down the side of the gully. "Any others?"

"Hit in the leg, Andy. Hurts." Sorenson was trying to find his gun, now ruined by the lucky shot. "Don't know if he has a friend."

"Let's get you back to the house and let Wanda and Mims fix you up." He half carried the wounded buckaroo up the steep side of the gully and got him on his horse for the short ride to the house. Pettigrew on the left and Austin on the right and they eased the man into the kitchen. The ladies took over immediately.

"Stay sharp, Mims. Need to find Houlihan and don't know if this fool was alone or not. Lock the doors and keep that shotgun of yours close. Where's Elizabeth?"

"She went to the bunkhouse to see if Jimmy Houlihan had simply come in and gone to bed."

Pettigrew and Austin bolted from the main house and sprinted all the way to the bunkhouse, screaming Elizabeth's name. Pettigrew was within fifty feet when two shots rang out, one throwing rocks when it passed between his feet. He jumped to his right and dove for the fence that separated the hog pens from the bunkhouse.

He couldn't be seen, but he also couldn't see and scrambled as fast as he could, all bent over and low, around the pens. There was farm equipment, including a couple of two-wheel carts, between the end of the fence and bunkhouse from that side, and Pettigrew made a dash for one of the carts. The move didn't bring more shots and he hoped that meant whoever was inside was looking the other way.

"Can't see anything, Austin. You all right?"

"I'm fine. Stuck under a wagon here. I'll cover whatever move you make."

Pettigrew snaked his way to the side of the bunkhouse and could hear what sounded like struggling from inside. Elizabeth was fighting off an attack. "You keep that fool busy, Elizabeth," Pettigrew muttered. There was a back door to the bunkhouse and a window next to it. He got as close as he dared and took a quick look inside the dark room. It was bright and sunny outside and that made it hard to see inside. Elizabeth had her hands tied behind her, but was struggling in the man's grasp, kicking out with both feet. Her fighting was moving the two slowly toward that back door.

Pettigrew checked, carefully, to see if the door was unlocked, and started to slowly get it unlatched and open. The door opened in and he had his revolver in hand. "Wrong time not to have my rifle," he muttered.

"Come on, girl, you know you want some loving from a real man," the outlaw laughed, still trying to keep Elizabeth from getting free. "You can't be happy being married to a scum Mexican boy, now can you? You need a real man."

"You're a filthy pig," she screamed right in his face and stomped down on his foot with her boot. Andy Pettigrew picked that minute to break through the opening door and rush the two. His charge knocked everyone to the ground and Elizabeth rolled free of the outlaw. Pettigrew slammed his revolver against the man's head and rolled back, jumping to his feet.

Blood was flowing from the outlaw's head as he reached for his sidearm. He was slow and died quickly as the big slug sliced through his chest, followed by a second round. "You're safe, Liz," Andy shouted, grabbing her in his arms. "You're safe." He untied her hands and held her close. Austin raced in and grabbed the now dead outlaw's gun.

She held on tight, sobbing softly, as he walked her out of the bunkhouse. "Mims will have you feeling fine."

"I was checking on Jimmy Houlihan when that foul man grabbed me," she cried. "Who was he? Where's Jimmy?"

"Let's get you taken care of and we'll find out. Two-dog's been wounded, too, so at least two men are involved in this." He, too late, realized that both of the outlaw intruders were dead. Who were they? Why were they there? Was Amos Warren involved? Pettigrew hurried Liz into the house and Wanda Camacho took over.

"I'm fine, Wanda, just scared to death," Elizabeth said. She tried to smile and found she couldn't quite do it. "Go find the others, if there are more." She let go of Andy's hand and sat down at the kitchen table. "Coffee."

Will Austin helped get Elizabeth settled, made sure she was comfortable, got a special smile from Wanda, and joined Pettigrew outside.

"Toughest girl in Nevada," Pettigrew muttered, climbing onto his horse. He rode toward the barn, planning to ride hard to find the others. "If Warren's behind this, he is one dead man, Will. My God, Jack Slater will hunt him down like the dirty dog he is."

26

Will Austin had Andy Pettigrew, Tiny Howard and Tubs Paddock with him on the search for Jimmy Houlihan and an intruder. "We'll go out the ranch road and start at the Skelton road for the search, boys. Don't figure they'd follow the path in, but it's a good place to start. Let's not ruin any tracks that might be there. Spread out some and remember there are two dead already."

Those words sent chills down their backs, raised already high anger levels, and added some juice to their desires. An attack on the Slater ranch? An attack on a Slater family member? Was it really Amos Warren behind the attack? Andy Pettigrew could see all of that in their faces. "Let's find Jimmy, boys."

Will was on the left and Andy on the right, with the two buckaroos in between as they moved slowly toward the big house. "Tracks," Pettigrew yelled out after just a few minutes. "Coming cross-country from Skelton. Looks like three riders, coming in abreast." Will and the others converged on Andy and they slowly followed the tracks in. "Headin' straight for the house, Will," Andy said.

When they were less than fifty yards or so from the house, two riders moved off toward the bunkhouse and the one stayed on track for the big house. "Tubs, follow those two. Hope they are the dead ones." Will said.

It was minutes later that Andy hollered out, again. "Bodies," he said. He stepped down from his horse and knelt next to a dead Jimmy Houlihan. "He was a good man, Will. Took a knife right through his heart, it looks like."

"This one's alive, Andy. Help me here," Austin said. "Jimmy sliced this old boy up good before he lost the fight. Recognize him? I do. Been with the Belafleur bunch for some time. Warren always favored him."

"Let's get him up to the house." Will signaled the other man, Tiny. "Ride hard for the ranch and alert the women that we'll have another wounded for them soon."

Austin and Pettigrew did their best to stop the bleeding and got the man into a saddle for the short walk to the main house. "Warren sent three men to burn us out, Austin," Andy said. "There's gonna be war in this valley. We gotta get word to Jack."

"It started some time ago, Andy. I'll take care of getting this gentleman to the ladies. I think you better ride hard for Skelton and alert the sheriff. I have no idea where Jack might be, but we need help, I think."

"Yeah." Pettigrew climbed into the saddle and rode off, spittin' tobacco juice into the wind. It was the fastest five mile ride he'd ever made, never once letting up on his fast cow pony. His first stop, an empty Burdick's house to rouse the resident deputy. "Paddock's store," he muttered.

"Burdick here, Valley?" He hollered coming through the doors fast. "Been a raid at Slater's."

"Back here, Andy. A raid?" Rick Burdick was sitting at the table with Valley Paddock and Jesse Winthrop, a platter of sweet rolls between them. "What kind of raid?"

"A deadly one, Sheriff. Three men from Amos Warren's place. Killed Jimmy Houlihan, tried to attack Elizabeth Slater. Two of 'em are dead, the women are trying to save the third one. Two-dog Sorenson was shot but he'll be fine."

Pettigrew had never talked so fast in his life, but he got it all out and grabbed a coffee cup. "Need help out there, Burdick."

"I'll say you do," the deputy said. "How do you know it was Warren's men?"

"Will Austin recognized one of them. Have you heard any word at all from Jack and the boys? We gotta get word to Jack. He'll be hard to hold when he finds out."

"Got a wire from the Elko office that they were riding toward Wells, chasing Three-toes Jacobs."

"I better send a wire to Wells and alert Jack about this. He's gonna be fit to be tied when he gets it. Can you head to the ranch. I won't be far behind you." Pettigrew didn't wait for an answer and headed up the street to the telegraph office to alert Slater of the raid. "Gonna take one of Two-dogs knives and filet that fat Amos Warren."

The train came to a jolting stop and Cactus Jack stepped onto the platform, his eyes darting back and forth, searching for Three-toes. Rob Slater raced down the length of the train to the livestock car to make ready if the horses were needed. Jack stood on the railcar's platform, also searching for Three-toes.

Three-toes was standing by the horse rack on the west end of the station house and waited for the train to come to a stop. He walked around from behind the caboose, up onto the platform, and saw Rob Slater running hard. He was too slow, but turned and raced for his horse.

"There he is," Rob yelled back at Cactus Jack, who waved for Jack Slater, and the three ran hard for their horses. Rob had all three out of the car and they were mounted, moving toward the west fast. It wasn't hard spotting the galloping horse Three-toes was riding right through the middle of town. It might have been early, but the dust was flying.

"He'll make for that road south," Jack yelled out. "Riding into Shoshone territory. We need to get him first."

Just as Jack said, Three-toes made a hard turn south. The Wood Hills were to the east, and so were the Shoshones. The tribe was angry at recent treaty losses and more than one person moving through their country wished they'd never tried. "Snow Water Lake? Or will he turn west toward the Ruby Mountains?" Cactus Jack yelled out.

"He knows the Rubies, Cactus, but those people know him, too. I'm picking further south. He'll try to make the Pequop Mountains, but we'll have him well before that. You have the fastest horse, Rob. Ride out hard. Don't wait for us."

Rob smiled and touched the spurs to that big cow horse he rode and Cactus and Slater had to smile watching him pull well ahead of them. *Three-toes is on a tired horse and I'm riding one as fresh as the day.* "Come on, boy, let's catch us a murdering outlaw." The bitter cold wasn't even in the picture as Rob saw he was slowly closing in on the fast racing outlaw.

Three-toes could feel his horse begin to slow. The pace had been too strong for too long. It was an all night ride from Halleck to Wells, and now, at a full gallop, being chased by the Slater crew. *Gotta find some rocks, a gully, big trees.* He spotted a large stand of cottonwood mixed with aspen and raced for them. He rode right into the stand and jumped from the saddle, his rifle in hand.

Three-toes found a jumble of rocks and dove behind them. The ground was wet, muddy, the air was cold, but his spot was well protected. He watched Rob Slater ride up to the trees and dismount. "All right you jerk, you're dead," Three-toes muttered. The distance was on the edge of too far and he decided to let the boy get closer.

Rob saw that Jack and Cactus knew where he was, and pulled his rifle for the pursuit on foot. The trees were thick and he found the ground muddy. *Spring fed grove.* He followed Three-toes horse prints, slowly, tree to tree, crouching low, watching for any kind of movement. Three-toes' horse was enjoying fresh grass and Rob saw a stand of rock and brush where the outlaw ran to.

The cold was starting to seep through sweat soaked clothing, the wind was picking up, and he was facing a known killer. "Easy now," he muttered. "Gotta be in those rocks, but can't see him."

He was as low as he could get and moved to his

right, into a thick stand of young aspen, feeling his boots sink deep in the mud with each step. There was a tangle of roots, mud, grass, and old leaves. While it made for quiet moves, it was also awkward pulling the boot out of the muck with each slow step. Three-toes lost sight of Rob and moved around his rock fortress for a better look and Rob spotted the movement. Rob slowly raised the rifle and took long aim.

He was pulling the trigger when Three-toes ducked down to look at something else. The bullet whistled over the outlaw's head and Jacobs dove into the mud. Rob Slater cussed softly, jacking a new round in. He moved closer to the jumble of rocks, spotted the outlaw trying to move back toward his horse.

"No, no," Rob murmured, and charged the ten yards at the man, diving at the last second, driving the two of them into the mud. Three-toes lost his rifle in the attack and pulled his knife, slicing at Rob Slater, back and forth, up and down, moving slowly away from the attack. Slater slashed at the outlaw with his rifle, fending off that shiny razor-sharp blade.

They were too close for Rob to try to stop defending and just shoot the man. He had to keep swiping at the knife. He made contact with Three-toes hand on one swipe and the knife went flying.

Three-toes tried to turn and run, but slipped in the mud and went face down. Rob stepped forward and drove the butt of the rifle into the back of his head, knocking him out.

He was pulling his face out of the mud when Jack and Cactus ran up. "Good job, Son." Jack said, helping to drag Wilson out from the mud and rocks. "Let's get this jerk back to Wells and get us heading for home."

"I probably shouldn't bring this up, Jack." Cactus Jack was leaning against a cottonwood tree, half a smile across his face. "The rustling, selling, and shipping of beef has been solved and the murder and robbery of Wilson has been solved and the sheriff hasn't been a single part of it."

"You're right," Jack Slater almost growled. "You probably shouldn't have brought it up. First thing I'm going to do when we get home is start a campaign to find someone to run against him in the coming election."

"Good thing I didn't try to shoot old Three-toes," Rob said. He was looking down the barrel of his rifle. "So much mud in there, this thing would have blown up in my face. Gonna take a month to get it cleaned up."

"It's gonna take fifty gallons of hot water to get you cleaned up," Cactus Jack laughed. "You're so muddy that fine old horse or yours ain't even gonna let you get on board."

They were still chuckling about the mud and chase when they escorted Three-toes into the sheriff's office in Wells. "Got a present for you, Deputy," Jack Slater said. "This is Three-toes Jacobs. I'm sure you got a wire from Sheriff Peabody on him."

"Came in this morning, Mr. Slater." The deputy got up from behind his desk and escorted Three-toes into a holding cell in the office. "We'll get him booked in shortly."

"This morning?" Jack looked at Cactus, Rob, and back at the deputy. "You sure you don't mean yesterday?"

"No, I got it this morning. Sent out from the Elko office. Something wrong, Slater?"

"Yeah, there sure is." He didn't say that the something wrong was the sheriff. "Peabody say anything else in that wire?"

"Didn't come from him," the deputy said. "Just a regular wire that the office sends out every morning. Sheriff's in Halleck as far as I know."

"This man is wanted on multiple charges including murder. When you get those muddy clothes off him, you'll find several thousand dollars he stole, as well. Hopefully, the sheriff will bring you up to date on all that."

Slater turned to his crew. "Let's go home, boys. No. Let's get the mud off Rob, find some steaks about this big, and then go home. I don't want to hear the word sheriff again for the rest of the trip."

They walked across the street to the hotel that advertised hot baths. "Cactus and I will be at the bar, Rob, having some cold beer while you get cleaned up. Then we'll eat."

A voice called out from the telegraph office down the street. "Mr. Slater, wait." The operator jogged up the board walkway with a cable in his hand. "Came in about half an hour ago."

"Thank you," Jack said. "This better not be from the sheriff." His anger was near the boiling point as he read the wire. "Not eating or drinking, boys. We're riding. Warren sent men onto our place. Jimmy Houlihan is dead and Two-dog Sorenson is hurt. You'll have to shake the dirt off when it dries, Rob. Let's ride."

27

Deputy Sheriff Burdick was in the kitchen at the Slater ranch talking with Mims, munching on a sweet roll. "Can the man talk, yet?"

"Hasn't said a word, Rick, but I don't want to talk to him, anyway. Is it true that the man works for Amos Warren? Can't believe someone would want to burn out a neighbor. Ain't natural to want to hurt someone," Mims said. "I sure wish Jack was here."

We have never done one single thing to that man. Why do people allow themselves to be filled with hate? Jealousy? Envy? Called our boy horrible names, tries to burn us out? Mr. Warren, you picked the wrong family to hate.

"I'm sure they're coming this way, fast. Soon as the doc gets through in there, I'll have a chat with that feller and find out what's really happening. How's Elizabeth holding up?"

"One tough lady, Rick. She's in there right now, helping Doc Whitney. She's got bruises and it wouldn't surprise me that she takes them out on that old boy." She had to laugh thinking about it. "A little jab here, a poke there, and she'd smile right at him." *I hope Rob understands just how lucky he is finding that girl. They latched onto each other the same as Jack and I.*

Burdick put the coffee down and walked toward the back bedroom, now a surgery. "Maybe I better supervise."

"If you're here to help, stay. If you're here to get in the way, leave." Doc Whitney was stitching one of many knife wounds inflicted on the man by Jimmy Houlihan before he died.

"Just waitin' for my turn, Doc. You doing all right, Elizabeth? I'll need to have a long talk with you, too."

"I got a couple more stitches to finish and you can talk to this piece of hog wash all you want. My oath says I gotta save him if I can, but it doesn't say I gotta like it." Doc whip-stitched a long cut as Elizabeth cleaned blood from the area. "There. He's all yours, Burdick. I was down at Warren's day before yesterday to check on his wound and the man's fine. There's something I don't understand, Burdick."

"Go on," the deputy said.

"Warren was involved in Jake Winters' death, shot the man after whipping him. Attacked the sheriff and killed young Delgado. Why wasn't he arrested? He's as much a murderer as this man right here. You have a responsibility to this community, Deputy and I want to know why Amos Warren isn't in jail?"

"My thoughts, too, Doc." Burdick wasn't ready for the question, knew it would be asked at some point, and didn't want to answer. "It's complicated, Doc." He shook his head, shuffled his feet somem and finally just said, "Sheriff Peabody would have to answer you. He never filed charges, is all I can tell you."

"That man doesn't deserve to be sheriff of this county. Any other county, either, as far as I'm concerned. Didn't file charges? My God, man, he got a man killed because he didn't take back-up that was offered and watched Delgado die." Doc Whitney stormed around, getting his instruments and equipment packed.

"I'm not a cussing man, Deputy, I don't get in barroom brawls, and I've never willingly hurt anyone, but your sheriff might be the first. This is more than malfeasance, it's complete disrespect for his badge, for our community, and Elko County. You tell him I said so." Doc Whitney was storming angry and walked into the kitchen.

"Coffee, Mims, before I hurt myself. Didn't file charges. Well. And a sweet roll to calm me down. Two, if you please."

Rick Burdick knew Doc Whitney was right and questioned his own position as well. *Sheriff ordered me not to arrest Warren, but I wonder if he really has that kind of authority? I was there, saw Delgado go down, knew Warren was at least partially responsible. Knew he killed his own hand. The sheriff is wrong, but what about me? Am I wrong not doing my duty?*

Burdick smiled a sad smile watching the doctor head out the door. He took a seat next to the wounded man. "You got a name?"

The man's eyes were open, filled with hate, shame, and pain, but he didn't say anything. Burdick reached out and jabbed him in the ribs. "Name," he growled. Still nothing. "Well, that's fine, we'll just call you Hog Wash. How long you been working for Amos Warren?"

"Who said I worked for Warren?"

" Might not know your name, but at least you can talk. Will Austin for one, Valley Paddock for another. Bought things from Paddock's store using Warren's account. Enough nonsense, Hog Wash." He scowled at the man, poked him again. "You're gonna hang for Jimmy Houlihan's death, so you might as tell me what I want to know. What was Warren's plan?"

The two men watched Elizabeth put her stuff away and slip out the door. "Well?" Burdick snapped

"We was supposed to capture young Slater's new wife and then burn down the house. We was supposed to teach her a thing or two."

Burdick tensed up, knowing what had happened at the bunk house. *This isn't a man, it's an animal of the worst kind. And he said Warren sent them. Peabody is responsible. Couldn't have happened if Warren had been arrested. Another three men dead because of a stupid sheriff and I work for him. My grandmother would not be proud of that.*

"Don't suppose that fat old man said why you should be doing that? Stupid is what I call it. Stupid is what I call you and your dead friends. Capture Rob Slater's wife and burn Slater out?" Burdick got right down in the man's face. "Why, Hog Wash?"

"Something about hating the Mexican kid is all I know. It was that kid that killed Sonny Belafleur. Also because Slater beat the tar out of the fat old man at the Cattlemen's get together. Said something about not showing a fellow cattleman any respect."

"You're worse than hog wash," Burdick said. "There ain't enough money in the world to make a man do what you fools tried to do." He got up, accidentally poking the man hard and pulled a couple of sets of cuffs. "Arms and legs wide open." He cuffed one arm high on the right side of the bed and one leg on the left. "Elko boys will pick you up when the doc clears you for travel. When you're standing on that scaffold, you look down and I'll give you a big smile, sending you to the fires of hell."

"You just gonna leave me here, like this?" Burdick didn't say a word, just walked out the door and down toward the kitchen.

"We'll ruin these horses if we keep this pace up, Dad." The three were at a strong lope on the main road from Wells to Elko and it was going to be a long ride. They would have to ride all the way around the north end of the massive Ruby Mountains before they could turn south for the road to Skelton and home. "We're talking two and half days or more."

"Trying to get the hate out of my system, Rob. Let's slow it down." They slowed to a trot and then a walk to let the horses blow.

"Hate? I'm more afraid than I am hateful at the moment." Rob said. "If anyone is hurt, then I'll fill with hate." *Elizabeth, Mims. Those beautiful little scamps. I'll rip Warren's throat open, rip his heart out.* He couldn't get the thought of his wife being hurt by that miserable man and could feel the hate building.

"I am already, Son." Jack looked over and saw the set to Rob's jaw. "Warren actually sent men onto our home to burn us out, Sheriff Peabody never put him under arrest for Jake Winters' murder or the death of Ricardo Delgado, and Peabody is the

reason we're a hundred miles or more from home."
They were miles west of Wells with miles more to
go and the frustration level was already high.

"We can make up camp on the west side of
Halleck, Jack and make it home late tomorrow."
Cactus Jack said. "Mossy Peabody started out as
a good lawman. Wonder what happened? He sure
made a mess of things."

"Got to feeling proud, Cactus. Happens to
people. Those parades through town with the
previous night's drunks and the cheering from
that morning's drunks." Jack had to laugh right
out at how he described the ritual. "Saying to the
crowd and to himself, 'Look what I did'. He was a
big man and quit thinking."

It was late in the day when they rode through
Halleck and were flagged down by the resident
deputy. "Good job, Mr. Slater. Sheriff showed me
what had been going on at that feedlot. Never
would have known it was a criminal operation.
He's over at the hotel if you want to stop in."

Jack Slater looked at Rob, then Cactus Jack, and
said, "No, don't think I will. Has he said anything
about the attack on my place?"

"Said he would take his prisoners into Elko
tomorrow and hoped to get together with Richard Burdick in the next day or two. Understand
Burdick thinks it may have been a couple of men

who work for Amos Warren."

"We better ride on, boys, before I lose my common sense," Slater growled. "Tell the sheriff I'll be waiting for him. Let's ride."

"I don't want to hear the name Peabody between now and when we reach home, boys. My focus is on Mims and the children and it needs to stay there." Jack Slater hadn't slept an hour, tossing in his blanket, getting up and pacing around the small camp, and now, getting Rob and Cactus up for coffee and sidemeat. "We ride in ten minutes."

"You've taught me what family is, Jack," Cactus said. "I never really knew until I tangled up with you. My blood is boiling right now, thinking of Mims and those kids you call scamps. You all are my family and when my family is threatened, I might just lose control."

"I'm so scared I can't hold this cup," Rob said. "Elizabeth," he almost was crying and sat down by the fire. "I rode off and left her."

"No, Rob," Jack said. He sat down in the dirt next to his son. "We all rode off to do something right. Something that needed to be done. It's a long ride we're facing, boys. Let's get it on."

Camp was broke, horses fitted out, and the three were on the trail in minutes. "We will need to spread the word throughout this county that we need a sheriff up to the job. Not a preening ignoramus. Men have died because of him on this little adventure of ours."

Rob looked across to his father, listened to what he was saying, but thinking something else. *He's talking like that to keep his mind off what he fears. Is Mims all right? Are the children all right? I'm riding in silence thinking the same thing. Elizabeth is so strong, so smart, and actually likes me. That's what's so amazing. I love her and she loves me, but there's so much more. We like each other. We want to do things together. I wish she was with us right now.* He almost had to laugh, but the fear of what they might be riding into wouldn't let him. *That old man called me some nasty names and now sends men to hurt my wife? Amos Warren, you're a dead man if one hair on her head is even barely bent.*

They got off the main road and skirted close around the north end of the Ruby Mountains, turning south well after mid-day. "Dust coming up behind us, Jack." Cactus Jack was pointing out a small cloud a couple of miles back.

"Scatter out wide, boys and get behind something," Jack hollered. He rode quickly to a stand of rocks, Cactus headed for a grove of cottonwoods, and Rob dropped into a still running arroyo. "Gonna get muddy all over again," he snickered. He rode across the small stream and tied his horse off to some scrub brush.

He slipped back through the shallow water and climbed half way up the slippery slope of the gulch. He could see three riders coming on strong and checked the load in his now clean rifle. It wasn't until they were a hundred yards or so out that Rob was able to see the shiny badges on the men's shirts.

He waited for Jack to make the call, the rifle at the ready. Jack let the three get a lot closer before he called out. "Far enough, Sheriff."

"Slater. Been trying to catch you."

"You ain't been very good at catching things, Peabody. Warren murdered Jake Winters and is responsible for Delgado's death. Been waiting for you to arrest the man, Mossy. Now, we've been told that Warren attacked my family. Killed one of my men. You ain't got a whole lot to talk about that I want to hear. We're heading home. You want to talk, ride with us." Jack stepped into the saddle and nodded at Cactus and Rob. "Let's go boys. Mims and the kids are waiting. You'd do well to shy away, Sheriff, we're running late."

Peabody was tired of beating himself up, knew he was a failure in Slater's eyes, but needed to protect his dignity in some way. He watched Jack, Rob, and Cactus start to ride off and nudged his horse forward. "Jack, please. I've tried. I want to be looked up to, I know that, but sometimes I just don't know what to do. So I make mistakes."

Slater turned in the saddle. "They go way past mistakes, Mossy. Your failures cost lives. Good men have died because you have failed to fulfill your obligations as Sheriff of Elko County. My family has been put in jeopardy because of your failures. You have men working for you who have time wearing a badge but you won't use them. You are offered help and turn it down.

"Ride back to Elko and turn in your resignation is my advice. Do something right, Mossy, before someone else dies. Your best bet is to not ride another ten feet with me and the boys." It wasn't a threat, but Mossy got the message, turned his horse, motioned for the deputies riding with him, and rode off toward Elko.

"Think he'll resign?" Cactus Jack watched the dejected sheriff's dust. "He's way too proud of himself to do that."

"I'm afraid you're right," Jack said. "Won't be surprised if he decides to run for re-election, but he'll face somebody with real strength, if I have anything so say about it."

28

Slater and the boys dropped off the main road into Skelton a couple of miles north of town and rode to the Slater ranch cross-country. "I want my arms around that woman, want those kids swarming around and making noise, want to smell the sweet smell of my cows," Jack said as they opened a gate letting them onto the property. It was getting dark fast and they were still a mile or so from the big house.

They topped a ridge and looked down on the house, barns, bunkhouse, and corrals in deep shadows. "Better ride in slow," Cactus Jack said. "Sure as I'm sitting here, Andy Pettigrew is standing near that barn door, rifle in hand, wanting to shoot somebody."

"Better start singing one of those Texas bawdy songs you serenade the cows with, Cactus. He wouldn't dare shoot us then." Rob joshed him some, but Cactus took it as a cue and started in on a cowboy's lament about losing a woman and taking to drink. He'd swear to the angels in heaven that the cows enjoyed the ballad. They were a hundred yards or so from the barn and Cactus was almost yelling out the words.

"Ride on in, boys," the voice called out. "I been watching you come." Andy Pettigrew stepped out the big doorway, rifle in hand. "Cows are sure to stampede if you keep it up, Cactus. Sure glad you're home, Boss. Been bad around here."

"Will you take care of my horse, Andy? All I want to do is throw my arms around that woman of mine." Jack almost leaped from the saddle and hurried through the barn toward the big house. Mims, Wanda, and Elizabeth were sitting at the table waiting for the crew to come in, great pots of food heating on the wood stove.

"Jack!" Mims was on her feet and in his arms, squeezing his neck almost to the breaking point. "I didn't hear you come in. You're home." He whirled around a couple of times, gave her a big kiss, patted her ample bottom and set her back down. He watched Elizabeth run for the door and smiled.

"Oh, Jack, it was terrible. Two-dog was wounded and Jimmy was killed. They tried to do terrible things to Liz."

"I know and I should have been here. Should not have ridden off and left you and the kids. I'm sorry,

Mims. I'll never do that again." Those thoughts had been eating away at him from the moment he found out Sheriff Peabody hadn't brought help with him back at the feedlot. How long ago was that? A year or two, at least, he thought. He knew then he had made a mistake. "Anything else since the attack?"

"No, but we've been at full alert. Rick Burdick has been out several times. He says that he can't arrest Warren. The sheriff has to issue an arrest warrant and that hasn't been done. He's going to quit, Jack. Says he can't look anyone in the face because of Peabody."

Will Austin walked in with a couple of hands. "Good, the boss is back. Everything go well?"

"No, but we got the job done, Will. Looks like you boys did a fine job here. Thank you for seeing to it."

Will walked over to the big stove and hugged Wanda Camacho, gave her a quick kiss and turned back to Jack. "Well, now," Slater said. He let a smile slowly cross his face, winked at Mims, and let Austin continue. Austin tried to give the impression of not paying attention.

"Amos Warren has hired some bad people, Jack. What happened the other night isn't the last of it. I think you've had a run-in with Cussin' Joe Pike. He's got two men with him at the ranch now."

"Yes, I have. Need to take care of the situation before it gets completely out of hand. I'll ride into

Skelton in the morning, Mims. Austin, you and Rob ride with me. We'll get Amos Warren arrested or dead. Peabody almost let Wilson and his gang of rustlers get away, too. He's a total failure in my book." He gathered Mims up again. "To think I almost lost you, girl." He buried his head in her shoulder and held on tight. "How are those little scamps of ours?"

"Asking when you're coming home. You spoil them terrible, Jack." She smiled into his face and got untangled from his huge arms. "I'll get them."

Jack, Cactus Jack, Will Austin, and Rob rode out from the ranch early in the morning, headed for Skelton and a talk with Deputy Burdick. "Liz said the men were especially looking for her, Dad. They didn't hesitate to say that Amos Warren sent them. The man needs to die. To be angry with me, that's fine. To take your anger out on my wife? There is nothing more wrong than that."

"You're right, Son. A man's family is all he has and evil people know that hurting a man's family is a terrible hurt. You can feel the knife slicing through your heart when your family is threatened. Evil, small minds, no morals. Those are the kinds of men who do that and they do need to be eliminated." Slater's anger had been building since he read the telegram back in Wells.

"Killing men like that is too good for them," Will Austin said.

"Is Burdick right, saying he can't arrest Warren?" Rob asked.

"I don't think so. I know I can stop the man, though." He had a grim look on his face, eyes were just slits, and his fists were knotted. "And I will."

They saw Burdick's horse tied up at Jesse Winthrop's stables and rode in. "Morning, Jesse, Rick," Jack said.

"Morning to you, Jack. Step on down and join us for some hot coffee. Glad you're back," Winthrop said. "That was a terrible thing Warren tried to do and old Rick here is trying to keep me and a few others in town from lynching the fool. He needs to die, Jack."

"I'm not in favor of lynching, Jesse, but you're right, the man needs to be eliminated." Jack tied his horse off and the five walked into Winthrop's little office. "One of the reasons we're here is to get an answer about why Warren isn't in jail." Jack looked at Burdick. "Can't go murdering your own hands and not go to jail, Rick. I just spent too many days cleaning up the sheriff's mistakes. Do I have to clean up this one, too?"

"According to the sheriff, he's the only one can authorize Amos Warren being arrested. He's as wrong as you can be, but I work for the man. What do I do?"

"You, me, Rob, Will, and anyone who wants to join us, will ride to the Warren ranch and place the man in custody. That's what you do. You then place him in your holding cell and send a wire to Elko that you are holding him."

"Can't make it any more plain than that," Jesse Winthrop said.

"He'll fire me, Jack," Burdick said.

"Good. Then you can run for sheriff and keep the whole county safe." Rob was laughing when he said that, the others joined, but Burdick seemed more worried about being fired than in taking a vicious man off the street.

"Rick, you're wearing a badge that carries some giant sized obligations with it." Jack said. He saw the man almost wringing his hands in self-doubt. Would he be the man Slater thought he was, or just another Mossy Peabody, strutting around with a shiny badge? "Warren killed a man in front of his own crew. He's responsible for another man's death, and he paid men to attack my family. How many crimes does it take before he's arrested? You might as well take that badge off right now if you're more afraid of being fired than you are of upholding the law."

Slater nodded to Rob and Will, put his cup down, and walked out to the horses. "Wire the sheriff that I'm bringing Warren in, dead or alive."

"No, Jack," Rick Burdick said. He stood up and straightened his shoulders some. "That's my job. If you men wish to ride with me, it would be appreciated. The sheriff is wrong. It is my responsibility to arrest a man who has committed a crime and Amos Warren has certainly done that." He reached a hand out to Slater. "Thank you. Ain't been slapped across the side of the head like that in a long time." There was a wry smile splashed across his face and Jack gave his hand a solid shake.

"I'm coming, too," Jesse Winthrop said. "He's brought some real slum-dogs in from Elko, Jack. Your people took care of a couple of them, but there are more at the ranch. It ain't gonna be easy rousting 'em out."

One of those slum-dogs was Cussin' Joe Pike, a low-life card shark. "If I remember the story, Jack, Pike had palmed an ace one night a year or so ago and you called him on it." Cactus Jack was chuckling. "Pike, more drunk than sober, had a little pocket pistol tucked up his sleeve. When he pulled the popper, he found himself flat on his back with a busted jaw, no pocket pistol, and no job."

"That's pretty close, Cactus." Rob joined the fun as they rode south. "Dad had Pike on the floor, almost standing on him, lifted his foot from the man's neck and helped him to his feet.

"I remember dad saying, 'Folks,' he was holding Pike up by his frock coat collar. 'This is the man called stupid. Hid an ace, got caught, and pulled a gun on me.,'" Rob laughed. "Then, Jack waved Cussin' Joe Pike's limp body all about. 'Time for you to leave town, Cussin' Joe,' he said, and walked to the bat-wing doors and flung him into the street. Jack Slater didn't buy a drink the rest of the night, nor the next day after cattleman meetings."

"You boys have your fun," Jack said. "Just remember that Pike also has shot more than one man. He's an idiot when he's drinking and a killer when he's not. Warren has to be expecting us, so let's serious up here."

The five men rode at an easy trot south toward the Warren ranch, each wondering if they would have to kill someone before the end of the day.

"Slater's back at his ranch, Mr. Warren. Saw him there this morning and rode here quick as I could."

"Thank you, Curtis. It won't be long and he'll be paying me a visit. Spread the word I want to meet with the men in ten minutes. In the barn, Curtis."

Curtis Belknap, a low-life drunk, small-time thief, known killer from Idaho country, ambled out of Warren's house to the barn to spread the word. "Gonna be killin' us a Slater, boys. Those fools Warren sent to burn his family out weren't up to it and got themselves all shot up. This time, we do the winning." He was always full of bravado until the first shot was fired, then found himself a hole to crawl into.

Cussin' Joe Pike spat some juice into the dirt. "Always got the big words, eh Curtis, boy? You follow Warren so close if he stops fast you're gonna get a new name. We'll call you feets, cuz that's all we'll be seeing."

Sandy Green had to chuckle at Cussin' Joe's thoughts. "When's this big tough Slater gonna get here?"

"Warren just said to expect him. Warren's coming out to talk to us." Curtis snapped it out after Cussin' Joe's comments. "Word I heard in Elko is Jack Slater is one tough hombre."

"Warren's skeered of him, I ain't," Cussin' Joe said. "Had one dealin' with the man. He's got one comin' from me."

"I ain't scared of nobody, Pike. Don't you forget that," Amos Warren said, walking into the barn. He had his quirt in hand, slapping it against his boot as he walked in. "There'll be a hundred dollar bounty to the man that kills him and fifty for the man that kills that Mex kid of his. That is, if I don't kill 'em first. Don't be waitin' for an invitation. You see Jack Slater or that kid, kill 'em. Questions?"

"What makes you think they're comin'?" Cussin' Joe asked.

"Cuz your friends didn't do their job the other night, that's why?" He was whopping his leg with his quirt, daring the man to challenge him. "He might be bringing men with him, but it's him I want dead most of all." He paced around the barn, looking at the three men, wondering if they were up to it.

Slater was big, strong, smart, and had never been intimidated by anything Warren had done. "Get in the loft, Belknap and keep a close watch. Green, ride out a short ways and if you see riders coming, race back to help us."

"I'll be in that grove of cottonwoods, Warren," Cussin' Joe Pike said. "When you ride back in, Green, get behind the cook shack there. Where you gonna be, Warren?"

"At the kitchen door with my double barrel shotgun." Warren seemed pleased and turned to walk back to the house. He had a secondary plan working its way through his mind, too. *After I kill Slater, I wonder if I can file on that land of his? That would be a perfect ending. I'll get even, finally, and come out ahead in the end.*

29

Burdick sent a wire to Peabody and joined the group for the ride to Warren's. They were a couple of miles out when Valley Paddock rode up. "Not sure what you boys are up to, but Squeaky McFarland just brought me this wire from the sheriff." He handed it to Burdick.

"We're riding to arrest Amos Warren," Jack Slater said.

"About time. Man's committed every major crime in the books." Paddock looked around at the posse Slater was leading. "I'd say you have enough for the job, but would one more be better?"

"Of course it would, Valley. You are always welcome to ride with me. Sure wouldn't be the first, time, eh?" Jack remembered a couple of times that he and Valley Paddock had ridden down outlaws. "It's sure to get nasty." He saw Burdick glaring as he read the wire.

"Something wrong, Burdick?"

Burdick handed the wire to Jack. It was simple and pure Mossy Peabody. "Under no circumstances are you to arrest Amos Warren on any charges. That is my job and my job alone. I am riding from Elko and you will join me in arresting the man."

"Going for the glory again," Slater snarled. *Just as I would have expected. Not a mention of bringing riders along, either. I wonder if malfeasance is against the law?*

"Your choice, Burdick." Slater continued. "Me and my crew are riding to Warren's place and putting the man in custody. You can ride with us, if you wish."

"I wish," Burdick almost whispered. *Peabody would shun Slater's help, expect me to ride in with him and face all those Warren guns, just so he could be the arresting officer.* "Yes, Jack, I'm riding with you and wearing this badge."

Jack led them to a stand of cottonwood trees where they could sit in the shade for a few minutes. "We need to ride in with a plan, even if we don't know exactly what we're riding in to." The seven men were circled, ready for the attack. "Rob, you take Cactus Jack and Will Austin with you and come in from open range on the north and the rest of us will come in from the main road."

"That's good, Jack," Burdick said. "Warren has three men plus himself and this will effectively split them up. Cussin' Joe Pike and Curtis Belknap are the most dangerous of the bunch, I think."

"No," Jack said. "Warren is." Jack led his group down the main road and Rob, Cactus, and Will rode out cross country to skirt around behind the Warren place. "Check your weapons as we ride, gentlemen."

Jack and Deputy Burdick led with Jesse Winthrop and Valley Paddock following. *If I was Warren I'd have someone out watching for us,* Jack mused. *That man wouldn't shoot but would race back to raise the alarm.* Jack was looking at all the places a man could be in order to see incoming visitors. *I would be in that deep arroyo that in turn leads back to the ranch.* Jack chuckled, thinking about it.

"Bet there's a lookout in Kelly's Gulch, Burdick. What do you think?"

"I'd have one there."

"Let's put the fear of the devil in that man. Let's ride right down that gully at a full gallop, gentlemen and watch the vermin flee." They all led their horses into the gully, running with about three inches of snow melt, and spurred them into a full run, howling at the tops of their lungs. Mud flew in every direction, water splashed high enough to drench the riders, and the scream would waken the devil himself. It was a Sioux, Cheyenne, Genghis Khan charge all the way to the Warren ranch.

"What?" Sandy Green was comfortably laid out in the moist, warm dirt of the arroyo's bank, watching the road that led to the ranch when the posse roared around a bend just thirty yards or so up stream. Green jumped to his feet and made a dash for his horse, losing by yards.

"End of the game, buster," Slater said, diving into the man and taking the two of them into the mud. Slater sat on Sandy Green and pounded his face three times before Jesse Winthrop pulled him off.

"He ain't goin' nowhere, Jack. What a ride. Ain't never done nothin' like that, ever." Winthrop almost yelled it out. "Who've you got there?"

"That's Sandy Green," Burdick said. "Slum dog. Tie him across his saddle. Might come in handy when we ride into the ranch."

"No!" Green howled. "No. They'll shoot me."

"Better you than me," Valley Paddock said. "How many of them lined up to shoot you, Mr. Green?"

"Cussin' Joe, Belknap, and the fat man, Warren. They're waitin' for you." Slater grabbed the man and threw him into the saddle, Jesse Winthrop immediately tied his legs together under the horse, and Valley Paddock had the lead rope. Green's eyes were darting from man to man, pleading. "They'll shoot me," he cried out again.

"Yup," Slater said. "Mount up, boys. This old boy's anxious to lead us in."

It was late morning, high desert heat shimmered across the vast plain, while great billows of thunderheads moved slowly south, their pillars of rain bent to the winds.

"Warren usually had men out patrolling this open range, but he doesn't have any men now that the Sonny Belafleur group is gone. We can ride fairly close to the ranch using the rolling prairie to hide us." Rob said. The hillocks offered deep draws and small canyons to ride through without being seen.

"Gotta watch for men in the barn, Rob. Warren's idea of a bunkhouse won't work for defending the place, but that barn does." Will Austin said. "It's a north-south building with a hay loft the length of the building. Man with a rifle can see for miles."

"Let's get as close as we can and then go in on foot. Wouldn't expect that." Rob Slater, Cactus Jack, and especially Will Austin, had been at the Warren property many times and knew their way around. "Let's keep that little hill between us and the barn and park these horses."

They tied off in a group of stunted pines and moved along the side of the rolling hill, well under the crest. Cactus Jack eased himself to the crest, flat on his belly. "We're a couple of hundred yards away, boys, but we can follow along the hillside almost right up to the barn."

He snaked his way back down. "Couldn't see anyone but didn't expect to, either." He said. "Should we wait for Jack to make his play or just go ahead and start our war?"

"No waiting on this war, Cactus." Rob had anger spread across his young face, determination, too. "I've been waiting for this day for a long time. My first bullets into that fat old man are from Elizabeth and the rest are directly from me. Let's ease around this fat little hill and tear Warren's place up."

Cactus Jack had never seen this side of Rob Slater and gave the young man a long look. "Don't let the thought of revenge eat your heart away, Rob. There's too much good in you."

"No, Cactus, there isn't much good in me at all right now."

That's just not like Rob. Cactus made up his mind he would stay as close to Rob as he could during the raid. *I ain't gonna let my best friend ruin his life trying to get even, trying to get revenge.*

They eased around a bend in the hillside, dropped into a cluster of sage brush, just thirty yards or so from the north end of the barn. The big doors were slid open and in the open loft, they could see the barrel of a rifle but not the man behind it. Whoever was up there would be looking more to the west than north, to where Slater and company were.

Will Austin slid back down the hillside some

and motioned for them to follow. "Rocky little wallow right down here," he said. "All kinds of junk thrown down. We can almost get right to that big doorway without being seen."

Austin led them into a muddy, rock and junk strewn wallow, around broken equipment, busted up wood, and rusted wire, to within ten yards of the barn door. "Get set, Cactus," Rob said. He picked up a large rock and heaved it at the open loft. The rock bounced off the wall just inches from the rifle barrel and the man whirled around, raising the gun to his shoulder.

One loud round from Cactus Jack's Winchester followed by the thud of the body falling from the loft and the three Slater men raced for the barn's open doorway. Curtis Belknap wasn't quite dead, tried to pull his sidearm and Will Austin kicked him in the head as he ran by. "Better keep an eye on him when we get inside," he yelled.

Despite the bright day and open doors, the barn was dark and the three spread out wide, searching for hidden weapons aimed their way. "Looks like we're alone in here," Rob said. "Cover that south door Will." Rob spotted the cottonwood tree just outside the barn. "Cactus, use that tree."

"Gunfire," Cussin' Joe Pike muttered. He was in the trees just to the south of the main ranch house, could see the barn, could even see Amos Warren sitting in that chair on the kitchen porch. He spotted Cactus Jack running for the cottonwood tree but couldn't get a shot off before he made it into the shadows.

Warren came awake at the rifle shot and also spotted Cactus Jack making his run. *Why didn't somebody shoot him? Where are my men? Do I always have to do everything around here?* He got himself out of the chair and holding his shotgun, was making his way to the kitchen door when he spotted Cussin' Joe pointing at the barn.

Rob Slater sprinted from the barn toward the group of wagons and carts near the kitchen porch. Warren pulled the shotgun to his shoulder and felt two bullets drive him back five feet and slam him against the wall. Will Austin pumped his rifle and let out a Texas holler that could be heard in Waco.

Cussin' Joe Pike could see the end. *Belknap must be dead, Warren is surely dead, and where is Sandy? Time to get out of here.* His horse was in the coral near the barn so getting to it was out and all he could come up with was to run for that big arroyo to the south. *Make it back to Skelton and steal a horse and get out of this country.*

He stood, turned to run for that deep ravine, and was met by four riders coming hard, three of them screaming at the top of their lungs. He stood, frozen, couldn't move, and Valley Paddock raced right up to him and almost took his head off with the barrel of his rifle. Valley, Jack, and Jesse raced to the back of the Warren house and ran into Rob, kneeling next to Amos Warren's body.

"He dead, son?"

"Not yet," Rob snarled. "But soon." Rob had his revolver in hand, cocked, and leveled at Warren's head. Nobody moved, watching, waiting.

"No." Warren wheezed, spitting up bright pink lung blood.

"You're dying, old man. You sent men to hurt my family. You went out of your way to hurt me." Rob's anger was becoming rage. "I'm not a good man right now. You have just seconds to apologize."

Warren coughed up more blood, his body arced in pain, and he whispered, "Never."

30

"I couldn't do it," Rob cried. "I put the gun to that man's head and couldn't pull the trigger. I've had such hatred for him, for what he's done, but I couldn't kill him." Rob was sprawled up against a fence post, his legs tucked up close, his shoulders bent forward. "He sent men to hurt my wife, to kill Mims, to burn us out, and I couldn't pull the trigger."

"Because, unlike Amos Warren, you're a good man, Rob. I'm mighty proud to call you my son."

The heat was fierce and Slater had four prisoners, two of them badly wounded. "We need to get Doc Whitney out here right away. There's no way we can bring these men to him." Amos Warren wasn't expected to live long enough to see the doctor, Belknap was questionable, and Cussin' Joe Pike would probably outlive them all. Green was just bruised some. "Let's move them into the barn."

"I'll ride for the doc," Valley Paddock said. "Elko newspaper will have a headline about the charge at Kelly's Gulch," he laughed.

They had a hard time moving the heavy Amos Warren into the barn, but the man was still breathing when they laid him out on some straw. Bright pink blood flowed with every breath. Cussin' Joe had a hard bump on the head and some lacerations and Slater had him tied, back to back with Sandy Green. Curtis Belknap took a rifle bullet into his mid-section and, like Warren, would probably die before Doc Whitney could get there. His eyes were already dull, his breathing labored.

"Let's get a couple of buckets of water," Cactus Jack said to Rob. Rob was leaning against the wall of the barn, his head hanging down. "I need to whup on you some."

"I wanted to pull that trigger more than I've ever wanted anything, Cactus. I was looking into those hate filled eyes and couldn't do it. I'm just not the man I thought I was."

"You're a far bigger man than you ever thought you were, my friend. Your man was down, unable to fight back. Only a real man would do what you did. It was the right thing to do. You were filled with this great demand for revenge, it was eating at you, but the real, the honest, Rob Slater is the one who didn't pull the trigger."

Rob looked up into those dark Texas eyes of Cactus Jack, straightened up, and smiled. It was a quiet 'thank you', and he wrapped his arms around his best friend. "Let's get that water. You have a way of whuppin' on me, don't you."

"I remember a lion wanting to eat me, Rob. You sure pulled the trigger that time."

Valley Paddock was just untying his horse, after alerting Doc Whitney, when Elko County Sheriff Mossy Peabody rode into town, alone. *A little late and understaffed. Just like Jack said.* Paddock walked up onto the boardwalk and waited for the sheriff.

"Paddock. Hopin' I'd find you. I want you to organize a posse to ride with me and Deputy Burdick. I'm going to arrest Amos Warren. Just another man or two will be fine."

Paddock winced at that statement. *Just another man or two? Jack Slater's stories about this fool are really true.* "No need, Sheriff. Fat old Amos Warren is already in custody. Me and Doc Whitney will be riding out to the ranch shortly, so you're welcome to ride with us."

"I specifically ordered Burdick not to arrest Warren. It's my job to do so."

"Guess you forgot to try to order Jack Slater around, eh, Sheriff? Got tired of having to wait for you to do the right thing and did it himself. Here comes Whitney now. Riding with us, are you?"

Doc Whitney drove his fine high-wheeled cart around from the carriage house and motioned Paddock and Peabody to get going. "Late again, eh Sheriff? Wounded men out there. Let's not tarry." He flicked his whip and set off for the Warren ranch. Peabody and Paddock followed.

"Injured men?" Peabody looked puzzled. "What does he mean?"

Valley Paddock scoffed, kicking his horse into a strong trot to keep up with the doctor. "It means there was a fire fight, Sheriff. It means men got shot. Hired guns from the ugly side of Elko were brought in to kill and burn Jack Slater. It means Amos Warren should have been arrested some time ago."

Paddock's anger at the lack of responsibility shown by Mossy Peabody was about equal to that shown by Slater. "Good men have died, bad men have continued to burn and pillage, Peabody, while you did nothing. This county deserves better, sir."

The rest of the ride was quiet except for the urgings of Doc Whitney and the entourage rode into Warren's ranch in a cloud of hot desert dust. "Where you got 'em, Jack?" Doc asked before the cart was fully stopped. Rob grabbed the lead rope and held the sweat flaked horse while Whitney gathered his black bag.

"In the barn, Doc." Jack pointed toward the barn and turned to face Mossy Peabody. "Your prisoners are in there, Sheriff. Go ahead and make your big show of arresting them. Better hurry. A couple might die before you get your chance."

"Where's Burdick?" Peabody swung down from his horse, angry on the one hand, fearful on the other. He had been berated by Valley Paddock, shown nothing but disdain by Doc Whitney, and now, Jack Slater was scornful. He'd take his anger out on his deputy, put his prisoners in irons, and head back to Elko, immediately.

"Doing his job, Sheriff," Jack said. He pointed again at the barn. "You are aware, I believe, that Amos Warren sent men to burn my place down and kill my family, aren't you? You're a little late to make the arrest."

Cactus Jack and Rob Slater moved over to where Jack was, knowing that Jack's anger was about to get the best of him. "Don't be shootin' the sheriff, Jack. He's just here doin' his duty," Cactus said. "Best get to it, Sheriff."

Rob nudged Jack toward the cottonwood trees just outside the barn doors. "Got some cool water over there, Dad. Sure sounds good right now."

Jack Slater had to laugh, loud and long, and settled down in the dust with a tin cup full of water. "Coffee, or maybe some of Horseface Hawkins' bourbon might be better right now," he said. "You're pretty good at tellin' your old man what to do." He couldn't hold in the chuckles. "That man, though," he said, nodding toward the sheriff, "is a total and complete failure. I'd like to just ride back home, boys, but I can't. Rick Burdick would be left with cleaning up this mess."

"Would if he still had a job," Cactus Jack said. "It might not be a bad idea for you to ride on home, Jack. Me and Rob, along with Will Austin, Jesse Winthrop, and Valley Paddock can take care of things here. I'm sure we'll be burying a couple of those boys in there and the others will need to be moved back to Skelton."

"Sheriff ain't bright enough to see that," Rob said. "Go on home, Dad. We'll take care of things here. If you stay, you'll get into it with Peabody and that wouldn't be good. Mama and the kids need you more than we do right now."

"I guess you're right," Jack said. He made a slow walk to his horse and mounted up. "Let most of the work fall to the sheriff, boys." He said and rode off for home.

"I gave you a straight up order not to attempt to arrest Amos Warren, Burdick. You don't leave me any choice but to relieve you of your position of resident deputy in Skelton. Hand over that badge, now. You're not worthy of carrying one." Mossy Peabody wouldn't dare to talk like that to Jack Slater, but to his deputy, anything was fair game. "Insubordination, that's what it is."

"Fool ignorance and malfeasance of office is what I call it," Doc Whitney said. "Burdick didn't make the decision, anyway, Peabody, Jack Slater did. Your days of strutting around like a bandy rooster are just about over." He was wiping blood from his hands, poured more water over them, and wiped some more.

"If you're here as the sheriff, I'd suggest you get to work. That man needs burying." Doc Whitney pointed at Curtis Belknap's body. "If you're here to cause trouble, get out of my way."

Rick Burdick had been standing near some straw and sat down hard. "Let me have some of that water, Doc. Been a heck of a day, so far." He looked up at Sheriff Peabody. "You can have my badge, Sheriff, but you can't have my manhood. You ever talk to me like that again, I'll break your jaw in fifteen places."

Burdick unpinned the badge and let it fall to the dirt, slowly got to his feet, and stood, face to face with Sheriff Peabody, glaring. He waited for the sheriff to flinch, which took less than a few seconds, and turned to Valley Paddock, standing behind the doctor. "Want to run my campaign for sheriff, Mr. Paddock?"

"I'd be honored, Rick. Let's make a wagon ready and help the doc get these wounded men back to Skelton, first, then we'll plan out your campaign. Looks like Amos Warren might actually live through all this."

"You can't just ride off and leave this body here," Peabody said.

"He's your prisoner," Rob Slater said. "Shovel's right over there."

The wagon was made ready, horses harnessed, but getting Warren's bulk in the wagon was the biggest chore. "Took the whole Slater crew to get him in," Cactus Jack laughed, closing the tailgate. "Can't imagine how much he might weigh."

The ride back to town was slow with Will Austin driving the team and Doc Whitney continuing to work on Amos Warren. Cussin' Joe Pike and Sandy Green were in irons, watched over by Burdick. "Not wearing a badge, Cussin' Joe, so go ahead and make a break for it. Just a simple citizen now and willing to shoot you dead. Mr. Green? That goes for you, too."

Neither man said a word for the entire ride in. It was a terrible chore getting Warren into Doc's place and in a bed. The two others were locked up and the Slater crew started the ride back to the ranch. "Peabody's got prisoners locked up and no resident deputy," Cactus said. "He's got a dead one and a wounded one, too. Anybody want to bet he calls on Horseface Hawkins to be acting resident deputy?"

"He might call on him," Rob laughed. "Horseface is way too smart to be taken in by Peabody."

"Got dust comin' up behind us, boys," Will Austin yelled out. They were less than a mile from the ranch. Rob moved off to the left while Cactus Jack moved to the right, well off the roadway.

"That's Ted Wilson. What on earth would bring him all the way out here?" Rob pulled his horse up and turned to meet his old friend. Wilson had a broad smile plastered across his bronzed face and pulled up next to Rob.

"This is a surprise," Rob said. "Good to see you, Mr. Wilson."

"Heard there was going to be a ruckus out this way," Wilson said. "Thought I better get in on it since I missed all the fun at Halleck and Wells. Peabody get Amos Warren all arrested and in irons?"

"Hah," Cactus Jack laughed. "Late again, he was. Warren's bad shot up, Belknap's dead, and Cussin' Joe and Sandy Green are locked up. Sheriff's trying to learn how to run a shovel, I think."

"Might have made a long ride for nothing, Ted," Rob said. "I know Mims and Jack will be glad you're coming, though."

"Let's get on to the ranch, then, Rob. The truth is, I made the call just to see you. You and I are going to have a long talk about your future."

"My future, eh? Interesting that I've been working on that for some time, learning everything a man can learn about raising beef, controlling water, and growing grass. That's my future. The Slater ranch. Liz and I are gonna have a million kids and raise enough beef to feed the world."

Cactus Jack gave out with a loud "Whoooie!" Will Austin laughed right out and Rob found himself blushing at his comments.

Ted Wilson, a big grin across his face just nodded. "There are others who may have other plans for your future, Rob. We'll talk about that over some hot coffee." The rest of the short ride to the ranch was quiet. *That man never comes all the way out with what's on his mind.* Rob gave Wilson a long look and couldn't hold back a big smile. *Just like with the packing plants and their shipping out large boxes of beef, he's got something up his sleeve. Talking in riddles is not a bad way to work through problems, but it gets tiresome after a bit.*

31

The long hot afternoon was almost over when
Elko County Sheriff Mossy Peabody tied his
horse off in front of the Alabama House Saloon.
"Horseface," Peabody said. "I could use a full barrel
of cold beer about now." It took some time to get
Curtis Belknap's grave dug and the man decently
buried and the day's problems weren't over.

"I guess Amos Warren's safe, but what are you
going to do about those two prisoners, Sheriff?"
Horseface set a schooner of cold ale in front of the
man. Peabody might be the sheriff, might even be
one of Hawkins' customers, but right is right and
Horseface didn't think the man's prisoners were
being treated right. He wasn't the kind of man to
not say what was on his mind.

"What's that supposed to mean?" Peabody was
tired of everyone in Skelton trying to tell him how
to do his job. "They're behind bars."

"Yup, they are that," Horseface said. "Hottest day of the year and they're in there without water or food. No blankets for tonight, either." Hawkins let out one of his fine cackles, hobbled down the bar and poured the sheriff a second schooner of cold ale.

"My God," Peabody gasped. "No, no, no." He looked around the empty saloon, got slowly to his feet, and walked out the door. *What is wrong with me? Are they right? Am I a complete failure? I haven't done one single thing right except for having the drunks locked up every night. I have to be a better man than this. I have to.*

Peabody made the short ride to the Skelton office of the resident deputy and found Rick Burdick packing his things. *Horseface was wrong. They have water. Burdick was sure to see to that. Someone else belittling me.* "I may have been a little quick, Burdick. I'd welcome you wearing that badge again."

"You are a little quick with your mouth, Sheriff. Not your mind. Only badge I'll be wearing will be the one that says Sheriff, not Deputy. Best arrange for these boys to be transported to Elko. They'll need to be fed, too. So long," he said. Burdick hefted the pack and walked out the door. His own cabin was directly across the street and he took up a commanding position in a rocker, enjoying the view of his former office.

"That was the finest piece of Nevada beef I've ever had," Ted Wilson said. The table was filled with Slater family, friends, and hands, and the platters were empty. "Got a telegram here I want to read to you. That's the real reason for this visit."

He fumbled in his shirt pocket for a time, coming up with a single sheet of folded paper. "I copied all the reports that were written from the Halleck feedlot episode and forwarded them to the cattlemen's group and to the governor. The cattlemen are already working with Elko County legislators to get those legal holes patched up."

"That's good to know," Jack Slater said. "Selling stolen beef should be difficult at best, but Wilson discovered just how easy it was. You and Rob figured that out."

"I may have recognized the ease of shipping cut up and boxed beef, it was Rob who figured out the rest. Here's what the governor said." He unfolded the paper and read the terse wire.

"Dear Rob Slater. Its been more than a year since we last met and from what I gather, you've been most busy. Well done, my young friend. Please consider this an official invitation from the governor. I would like you to come to Carson City and act as my agriculture aide. I have aides for mining and transportation, but not for such a large part of the state's economy as agriculture is. I will be forwarding a two-year contract that will include a generous salary, housing for you and your wife, and other benefits. Signed, Samuel Larkin, Governor."

Wilson handed the wire to Rob and sat back in his chair. "Cow boss for the Slater ranch, Rob? Or cow boss for the state of Nevada?"

"My, my." Mims said, so quietly it almost wasn't heard. She got up from the table and walked around to where Rob sat and grabbed the big man up in her arms. She held him tight for at least a full minute. Tears were streaming down her face. "I'm so proud of you," she whispered.

Elizabeth sat across from Rob and was staring at her husband, almost as if seeing him for the first time. "Is this for real?" Her young life had been so horrible for so long until she met Rob. Now, married to the son of one of Nevada's largest ranchers, to the man the governor wants as his agriculture aide? "Is it?"

"I can't just walk away from the ranch," Rob said. "I have responsibilities here. I have a breeding program that must be continued."

"Oh, yes you can," Jack said. "You have an opportunity to establish what agriculture in the state will be for future generations. It would be a long two years without you, but what an amazing two years it will be for you and Liz. Cactus Jack Faraday and I will do our best to maintain your breeding programs, Son and you do your best to make Nevada agriculture something we can be proud of for a hundred years to come."

Wanda Camacho brought a large cast iron kettle to the table. "Don't have a cake for the celebration. You'll have to settle for some of my peach cobbler, I'm afraid. I'll get the bowls and chilled cream."

"Let me help," Will Austin said. He jumped to his feet and walked to the counter with Wanda. "Ain't enough peach cobbler in the world to fill me up."

"This is all for real, isn't it?" Liz and Rob were in bed, wrapped in each other's arms. "We're really moving to Carson City? You're really working for the governor? All of this because you broke up a gang of outlaws at the ranch where my brother and I lived and we met? Mims has told me stories about how she and Jack met but I think our story is better."

"I think our story is most wonderful," Rob murmured. "I wanted to kill Amos Warren, Liz. I really did. I wanted revenge, spilled blood, ravaged body. But I couldn't do it. He sent men to do you harm and I couldn't kill him."

"Revenge would not have been sweet," she said. "Never forget what a good man you are. I'll never forget. I think we should name our son Carson, don't you?"

It was very quiet in the bedroom for the rest of the night.

A Look At:

Name's Corcoran, Terrence Corcoran:

A Terrence Corcoran Western

Terrence Corcoran carried a badge in Virginia City, Nevada until one day, in a drunken stupor, he shot the sheriff. Now he's returning to the Comstock looking to get his badge back and stumbles into a conspiracy that might put the sheriff, district attorney, and others in jail for a long time. A lovely working girl is brutally murdered, a Hungarian duke wants a Wells Fargo gold shipment, and the sheriff rehires him after first kicking him in a most tender spot. Corcoran was born on the ship bringing his family to this country, ran away to the frontier at an early age and brings his ideas of the old country and knowledge learned of the west to whatever mess he finds himself in. He's carried a badge, found himself in jail, and stands four-square for right, honor, and truth. You gotta love the guy.

AVAILABLE NOW

About the Author

Reno, Nevada novelist, Johnny Gunn, is retired from a long career in journalism. He has worked in print, broadcast, and Internet, including a stint as publisher and editor of the Virginia City Legend. These days, Gunn spends most of his time writing novel length fiction, concentrating on the western genre. Or, you can find him down by the Truckee River with a fly rod in hand.

Gunn and his wife, Patty, live on a small hobby farm about twenty miles north of Reno, sharing space with a couple of horses, some meat rabbits, a flock of chickens, and one crazy goat.